NARCISSUS

NARCISSUS

A NOVELLA

ADAM GODFREY

Shortwave Publishing
contact@shortwavepublishing.com
Full Catalog: shortwavepublishing.com

Cover design and interior layout by Alan Lastufka.

First Edition published May 2023.

10 9 8 7 6 5 4 3 2 1

ISBN 978-1-959565-05-5 (paperback)
ISBN 978-1-959565-06-2 (ebook)

For my lovely wife Heather and our children McKenna, Elise, and Teagan, through whom the world is a made a better place, and I'm made better for being part of it.

Insecurity kills all that is beautiful.

— DEMI LOVATO

"Mirrors," she said, "are never to be trusted."

— NEIL GAIMAN, *CORALINE*

1

Four lights grope the nothing. The plunging void ahead twists off into the dripping blackness like a limestone throat. From their vantage point, the cavern's mouth has nearly lost all visibility, winking from existence like a failing eye with the retreating day, bludgeoned purple-red by twilight.

"We're in Mykonos, Liam," says Ethan. He slows his stride and bumps the flashlight with his palm, shakes it in the air as if to dislodge some degree of brightness that the unit might be holding back.

"If I were a betting woman," says Kate, edging past him, "I'd say you're the type to press the crosswalk button more than once to make the light change faster."

Gemma snorts.

Ethan moves along without response.

"On vacation, three days in. That means we should be doing vacation shit. Ask me, this is pretty fuckin' far from that." His feet move faster as he fights to catch up with the others. "You hear that? Up there? Yeah. That's where *we* should be. That's the sound of life, good times, moving on without us, man."

As the stone drops, the catacombs have led them several hundred feet beneath the mountain surface. Up above, the voice of Grecian night is nearly shuttered from their ears now, rationed out in whispers from the neon venues that had rushed to life at sunset. The social crowd's begun to loosen, warming by the embers of their drinks. Their furnaces are regulated by a casual breeze which finds them from the nearby sea, not exactly cold, but cool enough to flatten any beads of sweat before they form. By now, the music would be moving them, turning underneath the lights, underneath the night. Down here, the air is hard and cold and holds the musky calcification of eons.

Liam stalks ahead, mindful of his steps along the ledge that once had offered ample width for tours. It isn't nearly as solid as it once had been, edges wetly sloughing off at certain points where moisture has crept in and loosened its integrity across the years. Beyond the failing edge a crevasse opens in the limestone like a wormhole, a black and patient vacuum running through the center of the earth and out again. Fifteen feet behind him, Ethan prattles onward like a restless five-year-old.

"And that car's a rental, in *my* name. Swear to God, man, if—"

Liam slows his pace, partially turns across his shoulder as the others close the gap behind him. "Ever see *Midnight Express*?"

"You serious? Let me put it this way," says Ethan, turning

fingers underneath his light. "Tried making my own cross joint so many times back in the day, I still got the burn scars to prove it."

Liam stops, slowly turns. "Not _Pineapple_ _Express_, dumbass. _Midnight_ _Express_. That old flick where dude gets busted at the border with a shit ton of hash strapped to his belly, ends up doing hard time in a Turkish prison."

"Real talk," says Ethan, "I can think of a dozen other situationally appropriate conversation starters." He unbinds a fist of slender fingers and starts counting off. "Favorite foods, music, movies, weed, who played Bond best and why Daniel Craig is the answer. Mentioning foreign prisons while trekking through a restricted cavern in a Greek national park ain't one of 'em."

Liam lays the beam of light on Ethan's squinting face. "Thought I might remind you where we are, what we're doing right now. You haven't shut up since we've been down here. Sound carries, brother."

Ethan peels away, throws a palm against the blinding light. "You mind?"

"Don't be a douche, Liam." Gemma shoves her way between them, jabs the muzzle of her light against his ribs. "Just keep walking. Nobody's stupid enough to be down here but us."

"And park security," says Liam. He drops the beam.

Gemma rolls her eyes. She holds her phone out, turns the camera toward the group. "Say cheese, bitches." The flash goes off and Gemma checks the shot, scowling as she thumbs across the filters. "Good God, this lighting." She brings her fingers to her scalp. "And my fucking hair. Y'all, seriously? Somebody could've told me."

"Just keep it down," says Liam.

"Look, I'm with Ethan. Can we just wrap this up?" Gemma slides the phone into the back pocket of her jeans, throws a glance against the darkened route behind them. "It's cold as hell, it's dank, and I'm pretty sure the best thing that we're bound to come across in here is the exit. It's like you're trying to live out some kind of long-repressed Goonies fantasy."

"Do you ever stop?"

"I'm serious, Liam. Let's go. We can still make it back to the rooms, get cleaned up, hit the bar. You know. . . shit *normal* people do on Friday nights."

"This place is cordoned off for a reason," says Liam. "The guy told me—"

"The guy told you a twenty-dollar story," argues Gemma. "He saw an easy mark. An American looking for adventure, and he sent you out on one. And that twenty? It bought a round of drinks that could've gone to us. A-plus, Liam. Way to go."

"God forbid we have a little fun, Gem," says Liam. He kneels and lifts a cuff of jeans, restores a sock that has begun to gather on his ankle. "Not that dipshit brand of North Carolinian fun you're used to. Something we won't find in a bottle or those shitty hotel lobby coupon books. Something other than fucking selfies and Jell-O shots, for chrissake." Liam stands again, checks his shirt, his jacket. He knocks away a stripe of powdered rock that's gathered on his sleeve.

"Fuck you, Liam," says Gemma. "You actually believe all that Narcissus crap? Greek legend, man. *Legend* being the operative word. Fairy tale." She kicks the fetal beginnings of a stalagmite rising from the floor. It reminds her of cypress knees protruding through the muddy gum lines of the Pasquotank back home. The country life she's tried so hard to leave behind, scrub from every fiber of her being, forget completely. Liam knows this, so he knows full well how potent his remark had been, the asshole. But she *had* gotten out of there. She'd done it, and done it on her own. She'd become the anomalous agent who'd escaped the run-down destiny awaiting her, just as it awaited all the others. Friends and family, no doubt still right where she'd left them, toiling at the registers of fast-food joints and body shops and kicking curbs of 7-11 parking lots and chucking empty cans of Old Milwaukee from the bridge on weeknights after shift lets out, pining over what they'd love to do in life, but couldn't for the list of reasons that would grow no shorter in the years to come. But not her. She'd escaped. Escaped the place, the people. The family, the nightmares attached. Things she never wants to think about again. She was doing it, whatever *it* was, as long as that old North Carolinian sand trap and its hideous trove of secrets had escaped the narrative of her future.

"Legend or not, I want to know what's in here. Accidents happen everywhere, but to shut things down like this; this is something else." He looks around. "I mean, this here is over the top."

The four of them had come in on a maintenance road, or at least what's now used as one. Wooden signs along the route stood partially decomposed, most of their adornments blanked by time and sun-wash. Only one had been preserved to indicate the route's restriction to essential staff. It stood watch next to a heavy chain, slackly draped across the entry point. The gravel road had taken them a little more than a half-mile by the time they reached a densely populated grove of trees, intentionally plotted row-by-row, an arboreal barricade concealing what had once been parking grounds for tour groups. Beyond the thirty years of growth, lines of trees with brush that filled the vacant ground between their strategically positioned trunks, an eight-foot wall of bougainvillea that had bound all sight from anything that lay beyond. Its chain-link endoskeleton had largely stood the test of time, though several sections had begun to kneel to rust and vegetative weight, enough so that the four of them had pressed it flat with little effort. They'd found the cavern hadn't been too far beyond, exactly where the man had told them it would be. Its entry crouched behind an unchecked screen of grass and saplings. As for their transportation, they'd managed navigation far enough beyond the roadway's edge before the earth had grown too soft to venture further. Concealed behind the outermost array of trees, they'd tucked the Fiat underneath some low-slung boughs of pine. There was little chance they'd be discovered there.

"They used to run tours through this place on the regular, all before that story hit. Some rumors, a little bad publicity, and they just let the landscape swallow up the entrance, forget about this place for good?" Liam shakes his head, unconvinced. "Doesn't add up. And dude at the bar? He didn't even really want that twenty. You notice that? I practically had to wrench the details out of him. Like even mentioning this place had given him the shakes, let alone telling us how to find it."

"Crazy thought, but this place might be shut down for safety reasons, Liam. It's a reach, I know." Gemma aims her light into the cavity beyond the pathway's edge and kicks a dash of stony fragments, watches them disappear from sight between the slabs of rock. She listens to them rattle downward like an endless game of Plinko till they've fallen out of earshot all together. Gemma ties her arms across her chest like a defiant teen and saunters toward him. "And old boy back there at the bar? Think about that. You come at him with a handful of internet rumors and a wallet full of paper and you expect him *not* to seize that opportunity with both hands and yank hard? You got hustled."

"Rumors, my ass," says Liam. "You read the same thing I did. You read what happened here."

"I skimmed," says Gemma.

"Facts, Gem. It happened. Thirty-two years ago. You saw the reports, the articles."

"Skimmed."

"Six friends. Gone. Like that." Liam snaps his fingers, punctuating his remark. He stops again and turns to face her. "The Sinister Six."

"*Sinister Six*," she mocks. "And to think of all the billions made from anti-aging products. Turns out the cure all along was a belief in urban legends. Why, one could stay twelve forever."

Liam stares at her, locked and loaded, weighing the benefit of returning fire. It was that or shut his mouth, take the hit, preserve the peace. Finally, he blinks, as if to reset what had come to mind, decidedly too harsh for use.

Gemma rolls her eyes. "Fake news," she smirks. "That's my take."

"Just another term for facts these days," he says. "Anyway, we're here. Give change a shot. Life's about more than liquor and losers."

"Well, damn." She hears the country drawl infect her words and cringes. "If you'd have laid that wisdom on me a year ago, you could've spared me those four feeble months we spent together last summer."

Against his will, Liam's mouth transitions to a subtle grin. "Touché, Gem. Touché." He turns, starts walking again, calls back to her across his shoulder. "But you're wrong. It was three. Time just moves slower in hell."

Gemma smiles, hidden by the darkness. But the smile is just as painful as it is pleasant. She'd never admit it, but she still has a thing for Liam. And in all honesty, he'd probably been on point with any blame he'd thrown her way. She'd little doubt she probably was the one who fucked things up between them. Her walls were lofty, utterly impenetrable, and she secretly hated herself for it. Hated her family for it. Hated her whole shitty upbringing for it. Something stirs inside of her, opens up her mouth to speak again, to keep the game of last-word tag in play when Ethan breaks the silence. She draws her lips together, swallows down the words that hadn't fully taken shape.

"So, this Narcissus cat," says Ethan. He leaps across three knobs of stone, reduced to childhood in the moment, whispering numbers to himself between each jump."

"He's doing it again," says Kate.

She'd kept mostly to herself till now, not wanting any part of their exchange. It's what Kate did. Observe. Blend. Stay neutral, conflict-free. She'd hardly realized words had even crossed her lips when Gemma throws a glance in her direction. "What?"

"The number thing," Kate mutters.

"Oh." Gemma eyes her steps, more mindful as the

pathway narrows slightly. The metal rail is still intact, albeit blanketed in rust, and she'd rather not be forced to use it if it could be helped. "Yeah. That."

"Some pretty boy. What's the fascination?" continues Ethan, his mind preoccupied with algorithms of obsession in his head, oblivious to the brief exchange between both women. Privately, he continues down the avenue of numbers spilling through his head in ways that only he could under-stand, mouthing them beneath his breath.

Eight, ten, twelve,

Divided

Sixteen

Two Fifty-Six

"I could take him." He throws the backside of his hand against the other's palm, snaps its hard vibrato out across the pitch.

"You have to be so damn loud?" hisses Liam. "The hell is wrong with you?"

"Narcissus was a demi-god," says Kate. Threatened with another round of childish squabbling, she throws the comment out like some diversionary bait. She moves a length of hair behind her right ear, carefully navigating polished tracks of rock, rubbed slick beneath the random surge of water that would overtake the caverns in the wettest months. But they hadn't been concerned about that, for now the only element that plagues them is the biting cold that gnaws them as they venture deeper underneath the surface.

The others turn their lights on her.

"What, like Maui?" Ethan forms a stupid grin and rakes the air with hook-shaped fingers.

Kate rolls her eyes across the darkness. "He was distinguished for his beauty. He fell in love with his own reflection in the waters of a spring and died there."

"So, he just sat there. Sat there till he died." Ethan dips his face, regarding Kate through upturned eyes. "Ain't buyin' it."

Kate shrugs. "That's the legend. One of many, every one a little different. A lesser-known belief is that Narcissus devoted so much time, so much love toward his own reflection that he offered it his very life, his very soul, and left his physical body behind in a bid for immortality. It's supposed to be a cursed place. They say his soul is still imprisoned there, trapped inside the waters of the pool for all eternity."

The group falls quiet. The only sound between them is the soggy crunch of grit beneath their stride. The hard air shifts, sweeping through the caverns with a guttural tone that seems to emanate from every stony orifice. The path has leveled out, opening to a wider base that's more directionally vague. From there, the cavern splits four ways like an aortic junction, several of those routes condensed to half that of the main, mere veins threading narrowly into the unknown depths. Edges of the main route bleed into a vague and borderless configuration where it runs against the wall and through, exposing deep recessions in the rock, too low for navigation with a set of limestone teeth that seem to bare themselves, denying entry even if they'd not been disadvantaged by their height alone.

Ethan stares into the blackness. He pans his light along the natural fence of thorns and bars. Shadows stalk the cavity behind the construct of stalagmites as they dodge the passing beam. He snorts in amusement, sends his stifled laughter scampering off into the blackness.

Liam turns. "What now?"

"Nothing," grins Ethan. "Just, well. . . I wonder what his pronouns were."

"You're a moron." Liam shakes the comment off and turns to face the path again.

"Alright, guys." Gemma claps her palms together, turns, starts back the way they'd come. She holds her phone out front, mindful of her footing in the feeble splash of LED. "Been cool. I'm out. Y'all have fun."

"Wait," says Kate. "Listen."

"C'mon, Kate. Not in the mood. I'm tired, my feet are killing me, and this is dumb. Added bonus, I'm also pretty sure my cycle's started."

Liam and Ethan turn away, whisper something underneath their breath.

"Let these assholes jerk each other off in the dark all by themselves." She takes another couple steps. "You coming with, or what?"

"For real. Be quiet."

A hollow note has risen from the shadows, low and mournful like an open bottle in the wind. An oily breeze moves through the group and seems to disappear beyond the teeth, sucked from the chamber with an effervescent gasp.

"You hear that, right? It's water," says Kate, stepping forward. She moves her light along the walls, searching for the source. The beam has terminated at a slab of rock that leans against the largest route ahead. It feeds the path into a lowly slung ascension, easily missed where they'd have otherwise been guided right along the long-forgotten tour route, following the steel rail off into a further dose of nothingness. The covert pathway cinches, feeds into a narrow mouth of only several feet in height, gawping black and empty. A plea of echoes swims up through the opening, almost interlinked into one long and lonesome note beneath a metronomic overlay of dripping water.

Kate turns to face the group, but doesn't say a word. The upturned corner of her mouth speaks volumes.

"Hell to the no," says Gemma. "*Hay-ell* no." The country drawl finds its way into her speech again. This time she doesn't care, doesn't even notice. "You've lost your damn mind if you think I'm squeezing through that." She wraps her arms around her torso, envisioning the ruthless press of limestone on her body.

Liam pushes forward, climbs a spread of stones that staggers flatly out into the clandestine branch of path, crouching to reduce himself inside the natural antechamber at their peak. He leans against the wall and lights the space beyond the gap, a crudely structured hollow in the limestone rock, undersized and moist with subterranean sweat. Though abused by time, the opening is precise, clearly borne of human engineering once upon a seeming million years before. Slabs of ruptured stone lay heaped about the base, remnants of an old guard to the chamber laid to violent rest.

"Holy shit, guys."

"What?" Ethan comes up at his rear, peering over Liam's shoulder. "What is it? Can you see what's in there?"

Liam doesn't answer. He turns a sideways shoulder, slipping out of sight between the walls. Ethan follows through the slot behind him, stooping as he wedges down beneath the low and ruthless angles of the ceiling.

"Nice, guys," says Gemma. "Real nice." She blows a shot of air and throws her eyes around the space surrounding, black gesso dressing everything the light declines. Kate walks ahead and climbs the slabs of stone.

"You're not going in there," says Gemma, the statement laid out like an order. "Right? What happened to sensible Kate? I want *that* Kate. Play-it-safe Kate. Homebody Kate. That's the Kate I need right now."

"Might as well." Kate moves ahead with caution, testing slicks of stone and grit with eyes on every planted step. "Came this far already. Besides, I'm a history junkie. You know that."

The voices of the two men stagger upward through the opening. "Get in here. You gotta see this."

"Don't do this to me," whines Gemma. Her typical demeanor has abandoned her completely. This is a side of her that Kate has never witnessed. Kate thinks of all the times she'd been discounted, left behind, played second string to Gemma's Type A, self-regarding bitchery. She feels something bloom inside of her. Something new. She feels good, in control for once. Right now, in this moment, she holds the upper hand. And in Gemma's pleading eyes, she could see the painful realization there, as well. And despite how steep the sacrifice, how sharp the blow to her ego, for Gemma, Kate could see it is a price she'd gladly pay for just a shred of her compassion.

Kate shrugs, throws her eyes to Gemma as she fits a single shoulder through the opening. "Your choice, girl. Coming or not?" And then she's gone, swallowed by the dark.

"Shit," whispers Gemma. "Shit, shit." She wraps her torso tighter, tries to shake the claustrophobia from her flesh, her mind. "Hold on. Shit. I'm coming."

2

Beyond the limestone mouth, the darkness opens wide and holds them in its presence like a midnight womb, bottomless and quiet, insulated from the outer world in not the geographic sense alone, but also time. The stone cathedral sings a song of echoes, every drip and breath and step a note that plays a dozen times across the void and melds into the next in anxious harmony. They stand inside a cerulean bath of light that stains the black, emanating from an abstract work of bioluminescence spackled out across the vaulted ceiling. Down below, a pristine doppelganger of the tapestry above repeats itself inside a pool as clean and still as polished onyx. While the air was cold before, it's something different all together here. The cobalt blackness seems to penetrate and spoil any outside warmth they might've smuggled in.

"Incredible," whispers Kate. Her jaw flops open, slack

with awe. She knots her arms against the cold and strolls beneath the subterranean constellations overhead.

"This is some legit *Avatar* shit," says Ethan. He marvels at the bioluminescent swaths that seem to shift on contact with his voice. His words chatter out across the chamber, shades of neon blue, light and dark that move like waves in parallel across the range of stone.

"What is it?" asks Gemma. "Is it moving?"

"Larval colonies," says Kate, eying threads of webs that hang like tinsel from the clusters as her eyes adapt to the natural luminescence of the chamber. Each thread grabs the light that rides its length, glittering as the four of them pass underneath the fringe.

Gemma backs across the floor, eyes the ceiling for reprieve, a futile measure. No portion of the surface overhead lay unmolested by the larvae. They are everywhere.

"Relax," says Kate. She turns to Gemma. "Just larval gnats. They're harmless."

"Right," says Gemma. The thought produces a chill that bullies through her five-foot frame. "Right. Larval gnats. Feel so much better now. Thanks, Kate. Thanks for that."

Privately, Kate smiles. She wonders what Liam might be thinking in that moment. If he'd maybe noticed her for once, recognized the fact that brains could sometimes overpower beauty. It's wishful thinking. A gratifying, solitary contemplation all her own. But truth be told, she'd easily kill for even half of Gemma's looks. Brains or no brains, beauty does, and often will, win out in most wars of attraction. And despite the fact that Liam and Gemma hadn't dated in a minute, the attraction between the two was palpable. It didn't take a genius to work that out.

Liam's long been moved to silence, standing at the edge of the pool, peering deep into its surface. He hasn't found a need to even turn his eyes above. The pool holds all he needs, and he marvels at the razor-sharp precision of the mirror image. The pristine capture of surroundings high and low at once, to include himself, staring back in such a way that looks as if the sockets of his eyes are gutted out and empty.

"Guys, get over here," he calls. "Come check this shit out. Fucking weird."

The others join him at the edge. "You seeing this?" He turns his eyes back to the water, throws a nod against his hollowed-out reflection. "Actually, kind of makes you wonder, doesn't it?"

The others find their own reflections in the water. They stare into the vacant sockets of their darker selves that watch them from the blackness in return, the backdrop pulsing like a sprawl of arctic embers just beyond.

"Something so immaculate. So unnaturally clean and undisturbed," Liam whispers. "So *beautiful*." His tone has almost taken on a dreamlike quality, far away from where they are and drifting farther still.

The four reflections stare back at their owners, hollow-eyed, superimpositions on a neon galaxy.

Gemma jerks away, two fists at the center of her chest. She looks to the others, back to where she'd stood. A sound crawls from her open mouth. A malformed word that seems to start before prediction of its end.

Ethan snorts. "Shit, Gem. You ain't *that* ugly."

"Shut up, man," says Liam. "Gem, what's up?"

Whatever trance has held them falls away. They all stare

at Gemma with the rudely awakened eyes of someone ripped away from pleasant sleep.

She lifts a finger, aims it at the pool. "It smiled."

"What?"

"My reflection." Gemma turns to Liam. "It fucking smiled at me."

Kate is staring at her still. Ethan rakes the backside of his neck.

"Stop looking at me like I'm fucking crazy!" Tears surge beneath her eyes, the first cut loose across her cheek and thrashed away against her palm. "I know how it sounds."

Kate springs her bottom lip, shakes her head. "Maybe *you* were smiling? Half the time I don't realize my own expressions."

"I wasn't fucking *smiling*, Kate." Gemma ties her arms around her torso. She looks around, a wildness blooming in her eyes.

"You just spooked yourself," says Liam. "It happens. It does. Just take a sec—"

"I want to go." The first mascara tracks begin to map their routes across her cheeks. "I have to get out of here. Something isn't right. This place. It isn't right."

"Legend," says Liam. "Fairy tale." The words fall with an added weight to reinforce their truth, careful not to break her nonetheless. He walks to Gemma, reaches for her arm, misses it entirely as she snatches it away. He takes a breath, clears an itch from the corner of his nose. "Your words, Gem. Just saying. Make believe. Remember?"

Gemma shakes her head. "I don't care. I don't care what I said." She fumbles with her light, turns it over in between her dueling palms, fights to find its button in the dark. "God damn it!" She shakes the unit, runs her hands along its length. More tears spill down her face. The flashlight rattles in her hands. Liam reaches for her, stills her arms.

"Whoa, whoa. Hey, easy. We're leaving. No problem. Really." He dips his gaze and runs it underneath her face to catch her eyes. "Okay?"

Gemma sucks a breath of air and nods. Liam slides the flashlight from her hands and turns it on, hands it back to her.

"Guys, let's go."

Kate and Ethan stand there at the pool's edge unmoved, eyes downcast on the midnight glass.

"Guys. Hey." Liam snaps his fingers, whistles. "Over here. Wake up."

They start at the sound, then step back from the water's neatly severed edge. They wear expressions cold and hard, disoriented for a moment. But then they seem to notice Liam, Gemma, and like a slipping gear brought home again, they catch up to the moment, begin to rise up from the fugue that held them.

Liam eyes them curiously. "Come on."

One by one, they slip in silence through the opening that had led them there. They find the path and follow it back to the surface. No one speaks the entire time.

3

Gemma sits down on the toilet lid inside her hotel room and folds onto her lap, cups her face inside her hands. She gulps down a full and milky breath of steam and lets it go. She does it again. She feels its heat release the wrinkles of her mind, a wasp's nest of disfigured gray that's ruminating on the night, the cave, the pool, the grinning face that was her own but at the same time wasn't. It's all so stupid and she knows it.

On the bathroom door, a knock.

"Gem, all good?"

"Fine, yeah," says Gemma. Her tone is strained, unconvincing. She sits up straight and reaches through the shower entry, dials the heat away from scalding to a less sadistic setting. The hanging steam begins to thin and part across the air around her.

"You sure?" Kate lays her forehead to the outside of the door and rests that way a moment. "Pretty spooked back there. Want to talk about it?" Guilt pricks its way across her insides for the way she'd treated Gemma earlier. Sure, Gemma has a bitchy side, but she's generally always been there as a friend. A damn good one. And then her thoughts of Liam. What the hell was that about? He'd always been a friend. Just a friend. Attractive? Sure. An attractive *friend*.

Kate's voice is barely audible behind the solid oak construction and the snap of shower water on the tile, and Gemma truthfully isn't entirely sure what's been said, but from the tone she knows it's likely in the vein of what she's already heard since they'd returned.

"I'm fine, Kate." Gemma rises from her seat and leans into the counter, reaches up to swipe away the haze that's blanketed the mirror. "Just leave it alone, okay? Just forget about it." She pauses there, eyes the woman staring back beneath the layer of condensation that already has begun to fill the path her hand had left behind.

"Stupid. I was being stupid. Just seeing things." Gemma gives a stifled huff. An indecisive cross between a nervous laugh and breath. She inspects her image, sockets bruised, seemingly recessed, hollowed out like sudden sickness. She lays her face against her hands and turns her palms against her eyes, shoves them up across her scalp. Gemma feels a chill slide left-to-right across her shoulders. It makes her wonder if some kind of virus might be working on her.

Opposite the door, Gemma registers that Kate is talking still. She isn't sure how long.

"Back there, on the way home," starts Kate. She holds her breath a moment, "Ugh. . . it sounds so freaking stupid. I might've seen some–" She stops, leaving nothing but the shower's hiss between them. "Gem, you listening?"

Gemma hadn't made out what her friend was saying. The words she'd spoken disappeared inside the flow of water, hanging like a firewall between them. But there'd been a question. That much she could tell. "Uh-huh," she answers.

Gemma drops the towel, bumps the shower door aside and steps beneath the stream. It cuts into her flesh, her muscles, melting down the knots of tension rioting inside. She shuts her eyes and tries to let the evening, the disconnected feeling in the hollows of her body slide away, find the drain beneath her feet. She drops her head and lets her long, brown hair fall down around her face, collect the water, send it to the floor in sheets. Kate continues talking. Her shapeless words are lost beyond the spit of water all around. Gemma puts her hands against her face and thrusts the water up across her forehead, flushed down the locks of hair, sent to the ground behind her. She clears it from her eyes and turns to face the back end of the stall.

Gemma seizes, muted like some kind of glitch. Her likeness stares back from a square of chrome, darkened features mutilated by the ropes of condensation running south. Laid across the slender hands of her reflection, a length of metal water line. She nearly turns and flees the stall, but something holds her there. It's as if the world has been reduced to just this moment. All else falls away, numb and distant. She can't help but hesitate, just the slightest bit, long enough to gaze back at the doppelganger in a crippling state of awe. It's all the time required. The line is lashed around her neck, snatched tight. Gemma's feet come out from under her, and the full weight of her body drops. Something crunches in her neck. It sounds like the rupture of an antique flashbulb and the room lights up to match, blinding white and agonizing. Gemma claws her throat, failing purchase of the water line. Her fingers open, close, finding nothing but her own, wet flesh where metal coils should have been.

Outside the bathroom, Kate attacks the knob and screams into the facing of the door. She hears the double-bass of kicking limbs against the tub.

"Gemma?!"

Choking. Thumping.

"Gemma!" Kate slings herself against the door. She throws her body's weight against it, making little headway with the European craftsmanship of solid oak. It thuds amusedly, shaking off the feeble effort.

All sounds have stopped. Nothing other than the lash of falling water can be heard.

"Gemma?" Kate breathes against the door. "Gem."

Something hits the shower floor. Heavy. Enough to rack a picture hanging opposite the bathroom wall.

"Gem."

The angry spit of running water fills the space, her head. Kate's hand rests on the knob, and through it feels a snap as the lock unbinds itself.

"Gem," whispers Kate. Her hands are shaking. "Gem."

Kate's phone is in her hand. She's already dialed a number, hadn't paid much mind to which. She's hardly aware she holds the phone at all. On the other end, someone answers. The voice is microscopic, buried underneath the pulse of blood that beats a violent river through her head.

She turns the knob, leans into the door. It opens, and a frantic cloud of steam escapes as Kate steps in. For the smallest moment she is blinded white. Nothing can be seen.

The only sound is water, an obnoxious, endless ovation. Kate reaches out and takes hold of the shower door, moves it to the side.

The steam has cleared. The space has brightened, come to life. The page around her is no longer blank.

And then Kate's world burns out completely. She feels her body falling, falling, turning over in the nothing that's rushed up to fill her mind, begun to zero out the vision that has struck her like a brick.

And she lets it.

Graciously, she lets it.

4

Kate can barely keep her eyes from closing, and her stomach still feels slightly ill. It makes her think of humid childhood summers and the belly bloat of too much water from an overeager garden hose.

An officer has finally walked her to the common area, provided her the personal effects they'd taken when they'd brought her in for questioning. She signs the offered form, swaps the clipboard for the outstretched plastic bag, her shoes, her purse.

She scopes the space, spotting Liam sitting at the far end of the room. An angry Coca-Cola unit chatters from its post beside him. He's talking to a woman, smartly suited, dark-complected, hard. Detective Sideris. She'd met with Kate already. Several times. The woman had been in and out, swapping places with her colleague every thirty, forty minutes over many hours, eight or nine, maybe ten. Time had run away a long time prior, leaving nothing but an existential smear where clarity of situation should have been.

Liam turns to find Kate standing in the doorway with her shoes stacked up in one hand, purse and papers in the other. She looks like kindergarten morning, waiting for a grown-up to provide direction on a daunting first of many days of school to follow. Kate can see that he's been crying, weeping grown man's tears, violently supplied. He comes up to his feet and stares at her a moment, then starts toward her, face red and billowed in the cheeks and sockets like a mat of clouds, angry from the storm.

She knows she probably doesn't look much better, and in that very moment also realizes she'd intentionally avoided her reflection this entire time, having no idea how she looks at all. For reasons she refuses to acknowledge in her conscious mind, she has no desire to encounter it. A chill drops through her body at the notion, Gemma's words still playing in her head.

It fucking smiled at me.

The detective Liam had been talking to is also on her feet. She trails behind him, now standing at his back as Liam wraps his arms around Kate's body, pulls her into his, warming her at once. They linger that way for a moment. Kate feels his breath beneath her ear, spilling down the backside of her shirt.

Sideris watches them. Her eyes are black obsidian, shining dully in the artificial lighting of the room. It seems as if she is expecting something. Maybe not expecting anything at all. Maybe simply waiting, just in case. Just to see what happens. Measure their familiarity, pick up on signs of being something more than friends. Give motive to the actions she believes Kate has committed, has failed at proving none-theless.

Kate looks past his shoulder, still caught in his embrace. The woman's eyes are cold and absolute.

"You are free to go, Ms. Porter." Her accent unfurls thickly from her tongue, but her English is exact. "I'll be in touch when we should need to see you once again. In the mean-time, we have your papers."

Liam steps away from Kate, turns his focus toward Sideris. "Papers?"

"Passport," says the woman. "A precautionary measure. Make sure your friend stays with us for a while, stays where we can reach her when we need her."

Kate's mouth opens, closes again, still parsing out reality from dreams, delusions, still working out how real this very moment even is, expecting consciousness to find her now at any moment, tow her back to safety. She could be in bed right now, head resting on a doubled-over pillow, morning yellow leaking through the curtains. It is possible. Kate nods to herself, willing it to be. Yes, entirely possible. God, she's tired. So tired. She shuts her mouth, doesn't even bother arguing. Kate gives Liam's arm a covert pat. She moves her head, barely even there, a lone, conceding shake.

Sideris stares.

"It's fine."

"So it must be," says Sideris. "I have your number, where you're staying. I expect we'll have no problems finding you." She reaches out, takes Kate's reluctant hand. The woman gives it one stiff jolt, holds it for a moment in her grip. "Understand, there will be questions. After all, I've never known the dead to tidy up." She sets it free.

Liam drops his brow, thrown by the comment. He takes Kate gently by the elbow. "Come on. Let's get you out of here." He glances at Sideris, force of habit nearly prompting him to thank her as they turn to leave, then thinks better of it.

5

"We should tell them," says Kate. She speaks through the open window of the rental car, allows the autumn breeze to flick the chestnut locks of hair across her shoulders.

"Tell them what?" says Liam.

"About the cavern," Kate answers. She sweeps a length of hair behind her ear. "The pool."

"You really did bump your head, didn't you?"

"Jesus." Kate whips left. "This is some deep shit, Liam."

"And it'll be some deeper shit for all of us if we admit to breaking into federal property." He throws his eyes on her, back to the road again. "You know this. God damn it. Don't forget where we are right now. We're not in the fucking States, Kate. They already have it out for us, but right now they're working with an empty gun. No need to hand them ammo."

"Out for *us*?" hisses Kate. "*Us*? Us *who*, Liam?"

He shakes his head, tries to speak but fails.

"Huh?"

"Look," starts Liam.

"No, Liam. No. *You* look. *I'm* the suspect right now. Me. Not you, not Ethan." At this, Kate pauses. "Where the hell *is* Ethan, anyway?"

"At the room."

"Nice. Real nice."

Liam goes into a half-shrug as he tries to summon some defense. "I know. He. . . he was having a hard time dealing. Toked up, then couldn't show up that way at the police station."

"Brilliant," says Kate. She leans into the door. "Where are we going now, anyway?"

"Back to the room. I already grabbed your stuff. At least what I could. Rest of it's roped off till they finish processing —" Liam stops, looks at Kate.

Kate's eyes are closed. Her lips are pressed against her fingers, shaking.

"— the scene," finishes Liam. "Hey," he says. "I know." His own voice begins to break, and he clears his throat to reinforce it, chase the pain away. "We're sticking together, okay? You're staying with us. Me and Ethan."

Kate stays that way a moment, nods, then speaks, an arid whisper. "Liam, we need to tell someone."

"Tell them what, Kate? Even if we told them everything we know without the risk of self-incrimination for the break-in, there's really nothing to tell," says Liam. "Not where Gemma is concerned. I don't know what happened, but—"

"Gemma said she saw something," says Kate. "In her reflection."

The compact car rolls to a four-way stop and Liam spins toward Kate, lays his left arm on the center console. "Level with me. I'm serious. Did you mention that? To Sideris? To anyone else?"

"No," says Kate, the briefest hesitation in her voice.

"You sure about that?" asks Liam. He glances toward the traffic light and back again. Still red. "Don't fuck with me, Kate. Tell me if you did."

"I didn't," she says, brow twisted. "What the hell?"

The light turns green, and Liam takes the wheel again.

"Liam," says Kate. Her expression clears, and dawning realization wipes the creases from her brow. "You saw something, didn't you?"

"Shut up, Kate."

"You saw it. You know she wasn't crazy."

"Kate," says Liam. "Drop it."

"I saw it too, Liam." Kate's eyes are wide and eager, waiting for his affirmation that she isn't crazy. That Gemma wasn't crazy. That there's something to this far beyond the realm of general lack of understanding.

He shoves a hand across his mouth, steals a glance at Kate and back again.

"I need you to tell me." Her voice is desperate.

"Tell you what, Kate? What? That we're suffering some kind of fucking shared delusion? What?"

"You know that's not true. You know it."

"What do I know? Huh? What else could it be?" He's breathing fast and heavy now, and his eyes are having trouble sitting still. "Think about it, Kate. Reflections coming to life, acting independently of our physical selves. Does that make sense to you? Would it make sense to anyone? Some shit you just keep to yourself. Some things are better left unsaid, unacknowledged. And in time, they go away, dissolve. They do. In time, it's. . . it's like they never even fucking happened."

"For me, Liam. For Gemma. If you saw something, you can't just leave it alone." Kate turns her focus to the rearview mirror, sees that it's been twisted toward the ceiling as far is it could go. She makes no mention of it, though she feels his eyes on her, on the mirror. "If you saw—"

"Yes!" bursts Liam. He strikes his fist against the wheel. The tears begin to come again, and this time Kate is sitting front and center, helpless in the presence of his desperation, his pain, yet at the same time comforted in knowing that she's not alone. "I fucking saw it, okay? You happy? That what you needed to hear from me? Goddamn, Kate. I saw it." Liam's hands begin to shake so hard they seem to fight the wheel. Kate reaches for his arm and lays her hand across the inside of his elbow. He turns to her, unsure what to say.

"What was it?" Kate's words come low and quiet.

"Shit, Kate. Probably nothing."

"Tell me."

"There's not much to tell, Kate. Damn it." He drags a huge breath from the cabin of the car, fills his lungs completely. She can see the tightening of his jawline as he fights embarrassment, the feeling of stupidity. Finally, the words begin to come again. "My reflection, it. . . it looked like it moved. Moved without me." Liam turns his eyes to Kate, moves them to the road again. "Anyway, that's it. Okay? I got the hell out of there." Liam cranks the wheel, lets the car glide left through an intersection. "I shook it off, and I got the hell out. So, I don't know. I don't even know if I really saw anything at all, okay?" He swipes a wrist across his eyes. "Just spooked myself shitless, that's for damn sure."

Kate stares at him, silent.

"And you?" says Liam. "What kind of batshittery have *you* experienced?" He tries to form a smile, failing miserably as it falls away into an unsupported, cynical inversion.

"Last night, on our way back to the hotel," says Kate. "My reflection in the window of the car."

"When I was riding you for having the window down, freezing us out?"

Kate nods.

Liam shook his head. "I'm an ass."

"Like you could've even known," breathes Kate. "I'd convinced myself it was just the lighting. The way it slid across the glass." She purses her lips, gnaws the inside of her cheek. "Tried to, at least. I knew that wasn't it."

"Seen anything since?"

Kate shakes her head. "No."

They ride in silence over the next several minutes before Kate speaks again. "What about Ethan?"

Liam shakes his head. "He's fucking stoned half the time. Probably wouldn't've noticed even if there had been something."

Kate manages a subtle laugh. "Good point. But more than likely, he's not even left the bed, or couch, or wherever he's sacked out."

Liam shrugs. "There's always the bathroom. Can't dodge that for long."

Both their smiles drift south again.

"What now, Liam?"

He shakes his head, keeps silent. They pass beneath a

sprawling grove of trees, shadows leaping through the cabin. The sun takes aim and fires shots between the branches, splashing them with fleeting bursts of color.

"Sideris says they found something. A message, written on some metal, a slab of chrome inside the shower." He glances at Kate. "I can't remember what it was. She mention that to you?"

Kate nods. "Amor te ipsum."

Liam frowns. "Yeah, that's it."

"Latin," says Kate.

"Yeah," says Liam. "Asked if I knew what that meant. Hell if I know. If Gemma knew Latin, I was the last to know it."

She folds her arms, tries to fight the chill that had begun to work its way across her flesh. "Took it back in my first year. Latin. But Gem, no, she didn't know it."

Her eyes are fixed upon the passing trees, breaking wide again, several homes emerging in the open stretch of land that rolls their way. She feels his eyes, though doesn't check for confirmation. "You'd better not be thinking what I think you're thinking." Rows of broken earth strum past and fade back to weeds again, the farmland left behind and disappearing fast into the distance as they move into another stretch of forest. In those early hours, the world seems prematurely winter-dimmed, slathered in a film of gray like night refusing change of shift.

"You know I'm not," says Liam, suddenly aware of uninvited notions that had snuck across his mind without permission. "I know you better than that, Kate." He hopes his tone is more convincing than it feels. Liam pauses a beat, watches a flock of blackbirds peel away and settle down again. The startled mass looks like a bedsheet lifted, turned back across the earth.

He glances at Kate. "What was that last comment all about?"

"What comment?"

"She said she's never known the dead to tidy up," says Liam

Kate lingers at the open window, watches the earth streak by. The morning air is wet and cool. "The shower head was hung in place," says Kate finally.

Liam frowns, moves his eyes between Kate and the road. "Okay?"

"Unless she put it back herself when she was done, no way she could've killed herself with that water line. That fixture wouldn't hold her weight. Not even close. It would've come down all together."

"You think she choked?"

"That's not really the question. Her neck had bruises, Liam. Same pattern as the water line, wrapped several times around her neck. No doubt *how* she died. Problem's that it makes no sense."

"Unless you're the one who did it," says Liam.

Kate turns on him.

"Not that *I* think you did," says Liam. He throws his hand up like a shield. "Not at all. Jesus. Just saying that's what the cops would think. What they're thinking now. Of course, that's not what *I* think." He turns to look at her, check the handiwork of his recovery. "You know that, Kate."

"So, what do *you* think happened?"

"I don't know what happened. No idea. It makes no

sense," says Liam. "But I know you didn't do it. You couldn't have. Understand that."

Silence falls across the car. Neither speak for several minutes.

"What does it mean, anyway?" he asks finally.

"It means I'm in deep shit, Liam. Unless they can figure out what really happened."

Liam shakes his head. "Not that. And we're not even going there right now. They're going to figure this all out, Kate."

"Then what?"

"The Latin. What was written on the chrome."

Kate turns to face the open air, receive the earthy odor of the fresh-turned fields, moist decay. "Love thyself," she answers. Kate turns to Liam, watches all the color leave his face as she repeats it. "It means *love thyself.*"

6

Along the line of surf, the air is swift and slightly chilled. The sand is cooler still, having discharged all derivatives of sunlight from the day before. But the rising star has just begun to peek above the ledge of ocean, spilling threads of orange-white over minor chops, slithering toward dry land. Up above, seagulls ride the wind, living kites that shout down at the early risers as they walk the stretch of sand and claim their spots. Though the temperatures are cool, slightly biting, it won't last for long. By noon they'll rise into the sixties, bringing with them larger crowds to eat up every vacant inch along the sandy bowl. On both ends of the beach, two mountains stretch out like a pair of slumbering dogs, guardians of some threshold, the space between protected from the wrath of open ocean.

Ethan throws the shoulder bag onto the ground and jerks the sand chair open, drops it at his feet. He'd been tipped off to this spot a couple days before. A local's beach, distanced

from the tourist districts, not so crowded. If it cut the likeli-
hood of shrieking children down to half, at least, then it was
worth the added twenty, thirty minutes that it took to get
there. It also guaranteed he'd get a little time alone. He'd left
a note for Kate and Liam, assuming Kate would come home
with him later on and wasn't left to rot in jail.

Assuming.

Gemma always had a tendency toward bitchiness, but
not so much that it might outweigh any good in her to
balance that part out, and Kate had never been so batshit
that she'd lay her hands on someone else. Let alone to actually snap so hard she'd take out someone in the mental blast.
Not Kate. Always bookish, always agreeable, Kate.

He'd nearly been up all night, mind rolling over and over
and felt he'd likely pop a fuse of his own if he didn't step out
of the nightmare for a bit, find a little time to get away alone.
He felt like Kate would understand that. Hoped she would, at
least. He'd see her soon. He was sure of that, and when he
did, he'd iron out any issues then. But for now, all he wanted
was some solitude. Some peace. Somewhere in that time,
maybe he'd come face-to-face with what had happened last
night, deal with any grief he knew was lurking somewhere
just beneath the surface. And besides, they were in Greece,
and though the circumstances weren't ideal, a secret selfish-
ness inside of him demanded that he seize the beach time
while he could. Before he knows it, they'll be on a plane back
to the States again, and no telling if he'd ever make it back
here in his lifetime. And on that front, he'd convinced
himself that it's what Gemma would've done if she'd have
been here, probably sitting right there next to him with
drink in-hand, assuming in that alternate dimension he'd

not be the one that's laid up in the morgue right now instead.

A range of gooseflesh runs across his body at the thought, and he drops into the low-slung chair that thrusts its metal legs into the sand beneath his weight.

Through the static rush of breaking surf, more voices can be heard now. Behind him, another throng of people trickle through the parted sea oats, emerging at the sagging bottom of the dune. At the termination of the shabby access trail, they break apart and scatter out along the hard-packed line of sand, wet and gasping in the push and pull of ocean froth. He begins regretting having not gone farther down the beach where crowds would be inevitably thinner. Instead, he'd dropped himself right here at ground zero of the access where the crowds would be most dense, clustering in a lazy lump instead of spreading out along the length of beach that ran for miles either way. He nearly stands and starts to gather up his things to make the move when something reassigns his line of thought.

A long and shapely Grecian woman, bronzed and smiling, is setting up not more than several feet out to his right. She lifts a hand to greet him. Ethan awkwardly returns the gesture, smiling back as she unbinds a rolled-up bamboo mat and sets it free across the sand.

A gang of figures tumble through his head. Calculations of the women of this year. Women that he'd been with. Numbers running January first through now, October third. Plain to beautiful, they all have their ratings, though he'd not assigned (yes, *assigned*) those ratings on a scale of beauty, but of essence. This year so far has totaled sixty-four. An okay number. Not great, not bad. If asked to explain this secret calculation in his mind, Ethan couldn't do it. It makes no sense, and he knows this. The numbers come to him on auto-fill, some aggregate of intellect, looks, stature, skin tone, hair color, attire, activity, perhaps the types of food one might enjoy, the topics of discussion they should choose. It could be anything, and as they interacted, that figure might evolve, fluctuate, slide left and right along that invisible, nonsensical scale. Ethan knows it is the sort of thing that might evoke some interest in his mental welfare, and not the good kind, mind you, prompting visits to the therapist or maybe worse. All he knows is that he has a fascination with numeric values of the world, or at least he'd fallen into some belief in early years that everything in life bears some numeric value. He'd inherited his love of numbers from his daddy, that very love the source of his success, owner of the largest corporate accounting firm along the eastern seaboard and doubling revenue each year since 2017. Yes, the love of numbers, though Ethan doubted that his daddy suffers such obsessions as he does. Of course, he likely wouldn't know it if he did. Whatever. It's his *thing*, and that is fine by him. Everybody has one, or so he figures.

Seven. This one is a seven. A good number. Solid number. I could use a seven.

Ethan turns his eyes back to the ocean, suddenly aware of himself; pasty white, thin, the antithesis of godliness, Grecian legend, American geek epitomized. And then, despite the Grecian beauty stretching out beside him, he wishes right now more than ever that he actually *had* gone farther down the beach where he'd not be so much a blinding beacon of male inadequacy as he feels there in that moment.

He steals another glance, playing off the move as if he's checking out who else is coming down the dunes, and finds her now without the shirt and shorts in which she had arrived, laid out in a yellow two-piece, her sun-glassed face aimed to the sky. The day is brighter yet, the air a little warmer than it had been only moments prior, and the birds that loitered on the wind have settled out along the surf and set to chasing tiny crabs that fight to mask themselves beneath the hissing grit.

He observes the kindergarten scribble of the waves, the far-off drift of some large vessel rimming the horizon. For a moment, all happenings of the night before are gone, and behind his now-closed eyes he thinks about the woman lying next to him. Older, more sophisticated, he imagines. Clearly, this woman is beyond him. Had there been a ring? He hadn't noticed, also doesn't really care. If she has a husband, he should be here. No, not necessarily. Maybe he's at work. It's Monday, after all. Isn't that what responsible adults are supposed to do? Hell, he wouldn't know. He's twenty-three, hasn't cut the cord entirely. They are on this trip on daddy's dime, and with the money that his family has, he truthfully wouldn't ever really *have* to work. He smiles at this. Even if the woman lying next to him is married, maybe he still has a shot. After all, money never leaves him at a deficit in matters of attraction, financial assets running laps around the physical.

Ethan feels the breeze of ocean slip across his chest, what could just as easily be the movement of a sheet pulled taut as this imaginary lover next to him rolls over in the bed. He feels the salted air upon his ear, the whisper of this older woman, her breath conducting movement of the finest hairs along his lobe.

Ethan.

Her hand moves through his hair. His mind is fuzzy, soft, euphoric. It isn't real. He knows this. But the daydream is so tangible he cannot bring himself to open up his eyes, summon truth to fantasy. Is he sleeping? He thinks this with a certain level of lucidity one might unexpectedly (often reluctantly) encounter in the midst of dreams that push the boundaries of believability just a little bit too far. An unwitting act of sabotage upon oneself.

Somewhere in the distance, out beyond the shore, the gulls have started up again. Commotion of the birds begins with one and spreads like flames across a mat of brush, raging high and frantic over some disturbance as the flock ignites, swarming in the air. Something brushes up against his leg, rough like sand. The sudden jolt undoes his eyes, and sunlight takes him by surprise, running through the center of his head against the backside of his skull. Ethan curses, coming up with one hand shielding sockets from the blast. Something bumps his leg again, this time the other side, lower, followed by a white-hot jolt of pain that makes him snatch his limb into the chair.

"Jesus!" He grabs the spot and squeezes, lost for detail as he tries his sight through stains of light that loiter in the center of his vision like a gang of purple bruises. What had done this was no dream. His leg is screaming, and beneath his hand he feels an oily slickness that has gathered underneath.

The fuck.

He feels panicked and self-conscious in the moment as

he wonders who is watching, who had seen him, maybe if they'd seen what did this. He shoves the backside of this hand across his eyes and blinks, grateful as the temporary loss of vision starts to leave him.

Gulls scream wildly in the sky. It reminds him of boiling crabs, childhood memories of his uncle laughing at the pity he'd expressed. The tears. He can hear the nicking of their frantic legs against the steel, quickening as they burn alive. He'd wept for them, harder as the screams intensified.

It's only steam escaping from their shells, Ethan. I promise they can't feel it.

His attention swings back to the spikes of pain, radiating from his calf. There is red. Blood. Lots of it. He can see that now in near-euphoric clarity as all his senses form a lethal edge, not the slightest detail sacrificed as he attempts to make sense of it all. He pulls his hand away, reveals a dotted arc of slender gashes. A perforated line cut deep into his calf.

Ethan sucks a breath and flips his leg. The pain has mostly left him now, anesthetized beneath a wave of panic surging through his body. The underside confirms an utterly irrational suspicion, a mirror imprint of the perforated line existing equal to its sibling on the topside. Only this runs deeper, purging gouts of blood onto the sand below.

A bite.

Ethan sits there in a stupid silence, further action stymied by confusion.

Asbestos packs his skull, and through it he can still hear screaming of the gulls. What the hell are they going on about? The thought is dull and ludicrous, a mental misfire. No. What had bitten him? That is the appropriate question. Damn the gulls.

Something runs against his lower back. Rough, impatient. Enough to jar his torso forward.

Ethan moves to stand, but his legs ignore the call. He holds his calf, looks around, finds no one watching. He pulls his hand away again and turns his palm against the sun. It shines candy-apple red.

Gulls. Screaming. Tangling.

The woman lying next to him has rolled onto her belly, sleeping. Her glasses rest beside her, folded on the mat. They are facing Ethan, and reflected on their lenses something isn't right. Something is off. Something is missing.

It is him.

The realization makes him ill. More so than the punctures in his leg. As bizarre and painful as the bite had been, the wound exists within the boundaries of his known reality. But this. His reflection, or lack thereof, it is a product of insanity.

The parabolic inverse bends the vision laid before it, spanning dunes to ocean. In the sky, the flock of seagulls loudly turns. Beneath is something else. Something jutting from the water. At first the image is too small, too condensed for him to tell. The woman's eyes are closed. He moves closer to the lens.

Oh, God.

Out in the water, Ethan sees himself. His likeness stands just several paces out, facing shore. The sockets gaze back black and empty, burned out like a photo run through both points by a cigarette. At the waist, there is movement.

Something butts him again. Hard.

Ethan throws an arm and turns, finds himself alone. Other than the woman at his feet, his closest neighbors are no less than twenty feet away on all sides, oblivious to him and what is taking place. He feels like one of those bastards in the movie *Ghost* when Sam discovered how to fight back from beyond. He grabs his chest, his waist, his legs, confirming his reality. At his calf, sand clusters to the punctures, caking where the blood cuts rivers through the grit.

The woman sleeps. In her shades, still folded on the bamboo mat, Ethan's likeness blackly stares back from the other side. At the waist, something thrashes, pluming red.

A jolt.

Ethan lurches, grabs his side.

Another jolt.

The sightless action yanks him from his feet. He hits the sand before the agony erupts beneath his ribs. Ethan wails. He feels an acid wrath consume the right side of his body. In his hands, pawing at a threat that isn't there, he feels his body's warmth explode. In the sand, his insides have unraveled, heaped beneath him as his thermostat runs cold with shock.

The woman has awakened at the sound and, facing him, begins to scream. It melds into the insane exclamation of the birds, rolling in the sky above the incident that plays out in the world reflected in the folded lenses. They'd known what no one else had known. A primal sense of evil. They'd known, had warned, had been ignored.

Ethan's body lurches on the sand and comes apart in pointed bursts of fury as the unseen mouths consume him.

By now the woman's consciousness has drained away, thrown her out across the sand beside him, flailing in her private darkness.

Ethan's body has gone numb. And as his flagging mind

begins to hitch and cling to slipping consciousness, it falls into an old, familiar zone of comfort. One in which it cannot help but lay the moment on that cryptic scale to quantify the pain, appointing one last value.

Forty-seven.

The number flashes in his mind, one last illumination on the backdrop of his fading world, gone to blackness all around.

Forty-seven.

7

The ninth-floor balcony of Hyperion Summit Hotel overlooks the streets of Mykonos. They form a lazy net that drapes itself across the town, unraveling here and there where rope-lanes trail off toward the blue Aegean, sparkling on the distant edge. The light of morning is a settled yellow, whitewashed and uncertain. Vespas rule the avenues below. They flit past the vibrant blues and reds and yellows of the vendors and their goods, most already having set up shop and readied in their chairs for business, some still catching up, but not too far behind and in no certain hurry whatsoever. Blotting out the lower range of sky, mountains nudge the sun, and the hard lines of their ridges melt away inside the light.

Kate is seated with her feet up on the rail, a steaming mug of coffee cradled in her palms. She hasn't drawn a single sip. She simply holds it there, deriving comfort from its heat, this artifact of normalcy. Liam sits with both arms tied across his chest, shielding him against a western wind that blows in from the sea. It smells of rain and salt. Kate draws the blanket closer to her chest.

"Can't believe his sociopathic ass," says Kate, squinting out into the morning.

"Don't read too much into it," says Liam. "Ethan's wired different than you or me. It's just how he deals. Handles things his own way."

"He left a note, Liam. Gem died last night. I was in jail, being questioned as a suspect." Kate repositions, shifting irritably in the chair. She jerks an edge of blanket from the concrete underneath. "Meanwhile, Ethan leaves a fucking note to tell us he went to the beach?"

"He's oblivious, Kate," shrugs Liam. "All I can say."

"He's an asshole."

"That too. Sometimes."

Liam reaches for the backside of his neck and drives the flesh around the muscle in his grip. He holds it there a moment, turns his eyes beyond the balcony again. Someone blows a horn below. A dog begins to bark. Several others join in, then launch into a frenzy as they catch the scent of grilling meat and onions, crossing Kate and Liam shortly after on the updraft nine floors up.

"This one time when we were kids," starts Liam, "like seven or eight, I think. There was this time we came home from school and went out back to play some ball."

"Long time you've known each other," says Kate flatly. She blows the steam across her mug. It fights departure like an angry ghost, rooted to the beverage.

Liam nods. "Know him better than anyone. Probably likewise with him. Anyway, we were out there kicking leaves around on the patio. It was fall, and his backyard had these giant oaks that pretty much buried everything beneath them. And so, my foot hits something in the leaves."

Kate is watching Liam now. She's finally drawn a sip of coffee, given time to cool inside her hands.

"I nudged it harder, kind of kicked at it, thinking it was something random on the ground. Bag of trash or something. The leaves fall off, and turns out it's his dog, this little beagle-dachshund mix named Chester that had been around since before Ethan had even been born. The kind of family pet that's more family than pet, you know? A fixture of sorts."

"What happened?" asks Kate.

"Freaked me out's what happened. I called Ethan over."

"No, to the dog."

Liam lifts his shoulders, holds them there. "Old age, I guess? Who knows. Just old, finally bit it."

Kate takes another sip.

"Anyway, I call Ethan over and he just kind of stares at it, you know? And I think it's kind of weird and all because I'm crying like a putz and it's not even my fucking dog."

Kate nods. "Right? What the fuck."

"So, his sister's in the house. She flips out, I'm crying, but here's Ethan, gone out to the swings and he's just kind of dangling around on there, winding himself up on the chains and letting go, letting it spin him, over and over and over again. Wind, unwind, wind again. Just went on like that for the next couple of hours. I was out there with him and all, and he talked a little, but wasn't quite himself. Fast forward to the next day, and he just breaks down in the middle of the cafeteria, can't even finish his lunch, and has to go to the nurse's office. Folks show up shortly after, take him home."

"Shit."

"Yeah," says Liam. "Shit. So, here I thought the guy was borderline sociopathic or whatever, but he was just processing things in his own way, at his own pace. So, point here is, don't take too much offense to him running off to the beach and all, okay? It's kind of just, you know. . . Ethan."

Kate nods, draws another sip. "Guess I'll have to take your word for it."

"Think of it kinda how cats run off to die alone. They don't want to be bothered. They just want peace and quiet to process things, figure things out on their own. That's Ethan. Ethan the cat."

Kate snuffs. Not a laugh, but as close to a laugh as the moment would allow. "Right. Ethan the cat."

Liam stands, stretches. "Pretty sure I haven't taken a leak in like six hours."

"Your business," says Kate. "Do your thing."

Kate hears the sliding door release and close again behind her. She sits there for a while and binds the mug against her chest, feels it's warm and constant breath beneath her chin. She watches the horizon, tracks the movement of a tiny skiff across the glimmering chop, hardly visible.

Inside her, a feeling has arrived from nowhere. A sandbag has been seated on her stomach, pressing it into her pelvic region, shoved down into her legs, her feet. Something's changed, but she isn't quite sure what. Whatever it is, it seems to emanate from deep inside. Movement without moving. Vertigo unprompted. A field of tiny hairs has lifted, bristling softly down her back.

Something else is with her.

Kate sits up, listens. Children's voices, shrill, foreign, speaking several floors away. A passing car. Farther out, a bell is ringing, small and glassy. She lets the blanket fall away and tenses, careful of her every breath.

Where the hell are you, Liam?

Kate turns to look inside, check on Liam through the glass. At first, she isn't sure what she is seeing. The disembodied sense she felt is suddenly before her, flung against the glass like surrealist horror.

In the glass is her reflection, only not. In the glass, she isn't seated. She's standing at the rail. The cavities that should've housed a pair of eyes are empty, hollowed out by shadows.

Kate throws herself around, finds she is alone, and the edge of the balcony is nothing more than it had been a moment prior.

Kate turns to the glass again. Her hands have started shaking so that half the coffee in her mug has been released, spilling down her leg, across the ground. It's hot, but Kate has come undone from all sensation but her fear.

The strange reflection smiles, holds its palm upright, and waves.

Kate is rooted to her seat. She cannot move, cannot form a solitary thought. The mug is sagging on her fingers now, fully emptied of its contents, burning on her leg, reminding her that she is there, seated, not standing, not at the rail, not—

The thing that isn't her has turned and lifted one foot to

the ledge, then the other. Its chestnut hair lifts on the breeze and rests.

The vertigo is back, sweeping through her. Kate's heart is raging for escape.

The likeness on the ledge then turns and gives a parting glance to Kate. The smile is gone.

Kate feels the mug's weight in her hand, looks to the glass, the thing that isn't her, sees it take a step.

She wails and throws the mug into the sliding door, in the process falling from her chair. The glass explodes, transformed into a sheet of falling crystals. With it disappears the image it had held, and for a moment all that she can do is reinforce herself for impact. She doesn't know if that has stopped it. Stopped the thing from stepping from the ledge. If it is on its way below right now, the concrete rushing up to meet it. To meet her. To break her body in a single sledge.

But that doesn't happen. Kate feels the raging of her heart, her breathing, the sweat cast from her flesh, and for the first time, the savage burning of the coffee on her leg.

Kate is plastered to the balcony. She cannot will herself to move, as if it might unravel some protective spell, the reason she is still alive at all. Liam stands beyond the broken pane, just inside the room. Kate stares at him, eyes wide and deep, utterly nonfunctional. She hears his voice, shapeless sounds that meet her ears without an ounce of recognition, coming from a million miles away.

Liam kneels, inches closer to her with one hand extended.

"Kate," he repeats. "It's okay. Hey." He snaps his fingers. "Kate."

Her chest pumps at a steady clip, lungs tugging at the air

with too-fast inefficiency. She moves inside the current of her swimming vision.

Liam brings his face to hers, fits a palm against her cheek to steady her. Her eyes seem to miss him all together, running up against the far wall of the room behind him. He moves his right hand to her shoulder, gently rocks it back and forth.

"Kate, talk to me. What's wrong? What happened?"

She blinks, a sign of life.

"Kate?" Liam frowns, drops his voice. "You saw something, didn't you?"

Something comes across her face, as if her soul has found its host again, reconnected with a solitary snap. She nods, still at a loss for words. But she is with him now, understanding him completely.

"It was in the glass, wasn't it? Your reflection. You saw it."

Tears fall across her cheeks. She nods again, at first uncertain, unwilling to commit completely to the insanity of what she saw, then lets go completely as her voice begins to find its way into the open. She begins to break down all together. "I saw it. It's real. It was here, Liam. I saw it."

"Come here," motions Liam. He takes Kate by the arms and pulls her close, begins to lift her to her feet. "Come on. Let's get out of here."

"Where? Where are we going?"

"There's someone we need to find. Someone we need to talk to."

"Nobody's going to believe us, Liam."

"I can think of someone who might."

8

The '91 Audi 200 climbs the mountain road on the same, persistent note of the VHS tape rewinder Liam's parents kept in plain sight on the TV console like some weapon of embarrassment. Its usage always seemed to come with great intent. His father seemed to task the unit only in the presence of Liam's friends, a hellish conversation starter that would always lead to reminiscence of the *good ole days* of video stores and rentals and how the movie scene just ain't the same these days. The thing would reel into a high-pitched whine that filled the downstairs quarters, sounding like at any moment friction of the plastic rotors was about to launch into kinetic flameworks.

He pictures something similar happening to the car's transmission as it powers them uphill. The driver, however, seems adequately unconcerned, well-acquainted with the limitations of his antiquated transport.

They could've taken their own car, but that would put them up front with the mirrors and reflective panels of the dash and doors. It all seemed so damn idiotic. Even still, he and Kate had both encountered darker versions of themselves, insane as it may be, by now convinced they're tossed into the deep end of the universe, far beyond the boundaries of their understanding. He can only hope the one they plan to visit holds some kind of explanation, can maybe offer them some kind of help. In the meantime, the only thing in their control is their exposure to their own reflections. And for now, that means calling in a ride, sitting in the back seat, away from reflective surfaces of any kind. Even all four windows had been rolled down. They'd offered the driver another ten for doing so, and before he'd picked them up, ensured they'd been down in advance of their approach. The paint itself was even matte in finish, entirely unreflective, the older model vehicle a special inquiry that Liam made when the call was put out. This had confused the man on the other end of the line considerably, but Liam was persistent, patient, and in the end succeeded in fulfillment of his strange request. It was exactly what he'd ordered, despite the added angst he'd gotten from the antique's struggle up the mountain's side.

Liam keeps an eye on Kate, unsure how she's doing, doubtful she'd been tuned in enough to pay much mind to their surroundings. She sits with her hands plunged in between her thighs, eyes tucked in beside them.

"Hey," whispers Liam.

Kate offers him a single nod, face down. "Hey, yourself."

"Gonna figure this out, okay?"

"Sure we are."

"I'm serious. This guy, he's still around for a reason, right?"

Kate grunts, nods again. "In the meantime, all we have to do is stay clear of our own reflections, right?" She begins to laugh, no more than a clicking sound that rises up from deep inside and rattles in her chest. Kate seals her eyes, seems to lose herself inside the private joke.

"Kate. Gotta hang in there, okay? We really are going to figure this thing out."

She doesn't seem to hear him. "I mean, how hard can it be? Only just about everything has a reflective surface. Cell phones, rain puddles, glass, chrome, doorknobs. How about our own eyes? Those are shiny too. Maybe we shouldn't look at one another, maybe even close them all together, wander blindly around town. Shit." Kate brings her hands up to her face and shoves her fingers deep into her sockets, holds them there a moment till her vision ceases sparking in the darkness.

Liam calls up to the driver. "What's our ETA?"

"Our what you say?"

"Sorry," says Liam. "Time. How much longer? How many minutes?"

"Ten, maybe."

The mountain road has leveled out a bit, and the Audi's engine has relaxed into a less ambitious hum. The view out to their left is unobstructed, open air and sea with dots of homes and other buildings peppered out across the closer range of earth. Looking down, they feel the road has taken them much higher than it initially had appeared at base level. The homes up here are scarce, sparsely scattered here and there with mostly crags of rock and brush dividing them.

Groves of pine and fir, patched across the surface of the hills at lower altitudes, had begun to form a closely knit configuration at the mountain's upper regions. Light and shadow flicker through the inside of the Audi as they pass beneath the branches, a kaleidoscopic dance of yin and yang, good and evil. The movement of the car and of the light begin to turn Kate's stomach, and she crams her hands between her legs a little harder, tries not to focus on the rising tide of sweat that's now begun to breach her flesh. She lets out a breath, at the same time just the smallest sound that captures Liam's focus.

"Almost there. You good?"

Kate nods. Liam gently takes her by the arm and slips her hand out from between her legs. He takes it in his own and squeezes. The gesture isn't much, yet seems enough to move the vertigo to some abandoned closet in a back room of her mind. Her thoughts are on her hand in his now. It feels good.

The driver wheels the car onto an asphalt drive that takes a sudden lurch uphill, an angle that feels every bit of forty-five degrees. The Audi's engine bursts into a ghastly, heated whine that seems to ride the chassis through the seats and fill their bodies with a thousand buzzing flies. The light and shadows crawl across them slowly now, then freeze and slide from sight, banished as they level out across the driveway's peak. Through the open windows, now that the engine's voice has calmed, they can only hear the gnash of gravel under tires, birdsong echo through the timber, somewhere out beyond the canopy of leaves above, a jetliner's descent into Mykonos International. The air is cool and smells of newborn rain, organic dampness, of life in its most rudimentary form.

"We are here," belts the driver. In his heavy southeastern European accent, it's almost a celebratory exclamation. He reaches for the mirror in a move to situate it on his backseat passengers, then stops before they can respond. "Ah! No mirror, no reflection. I almost forget!" He smiles. "But, the sun. Not so much I can do about that, as you see." He waves his right hand through the air and laughs good-naturedly at his own joke.

Liam smiles politely back. "We'll manage. No worries."

He pops the door, lays one foot on the gravel drive. "Can you wait for us?"

"Sure. I wait. Time and money, though. You know, yes?"

"We'll pay, of course."

"Then I wait as long as you need, my friend." The driver winks. "While I wait, I eat." He holds up a bag and lays it on the seat beside him.

Liam nods, then gives Kate's hand a tug. "Come on. Just hope we got the right place, right guy."

The two step out onto the drive and sling the car door shut. The home is small, a basic unit that could be no more than 800 or 900 square feet in size, the roof a mat of needles from the trees surrounding, though its porch, a grounded slab of concrete, is freshly swept, well-maintained with a weather-beaten rocker to the right side of the door. In one corner is an old-school charcoal Weber with a half-rolled bag of briquettes wedged against its leg. They've not yet reached the porch before the door swings open and a man steps out, firmly built and somewhere in his fifties, maybe sixties. He keeps one hand hitched behind his back, a gun no doubt inside its palm. His brow is knit into a cautious question as he steps beyond the threshold, pulls shut the door behind him.

"Help you?" His eyes walk from Kate to Liam, back to Kate again. Only once does he pay notice to the idling Audi and its driver farther out, a fleeting glance.

"We hoped to speak with you."

"I think you have the wrong house," says the man.

"Are you Sebastian Drivas?" Liam catches himself, steps toward the man with hand extended. "I'm sorry. My name's Liam. This is Kate.

The man looks at the outstretched hand, at Kate, then turns his focus back to Liam. He leaves the young man's hand outstretched before him. Liam sees the man's arm flex behind his back, affirmation of his weapon's grip, whatever he is holding. At last, the large man nods, the slightest dip of chin. "Yes. But there are many Drivas homes in Mykonos, I assure you."

Liam drops his hand. "About thirty years ago, you lost some friends of yours."

The man's jaw tightens and releases.

"We should probably go, Liam," whispers Kate. "Let him be."

"Next month makes thirty-two," mumbles Drivas. "Why are you here? And what interest do you have in that?"

"There was a cavern," says Liam, taking one step closer. "Seven of you went in. You brought something back with you."

"What do you know?" says the man.

"I know no one believed you."

"And you do?" The man lets out a laugh, shoves a fist across his nose, sighs amusedly. "And what? Who are you?

Some ghost hunter, trolling the internet for stories? Last time one of you came through, I had to get very firm, make myself very clear. My clarity has dimmed, it seems." He takes a step toward Liam."

"Mr. Drivas, that's not why we're here. We're here because we need your help."

"My help," says Drivas. "What exactly can I do for you?"

"There were seven of you," says Liam. "Six died. You survived. We need to know how."

Drivas stops, lets his arm fall from behind his back. In his hand he holds a matte black Sig Sauer P250. In the car, their driver has stopped chewing, lips fringed by threads of lettuce. Liam turns to him, holds up a palm of reassurance.

"What have you done?" asks Drivas. "What have you brought here to my home?" His large frame begins to shake, and any curiosity has left his eyes. It seems the earth should soon begin to shift in unison. Threadbare fear has fallen in to take its place.

"We haven't come to hurt you, to scare you, nothing like that."

"That's no longer in your hands. It's not your choice. You have no idea."

"We need your help. Talk to us. Please."

"When did you find the pool?" asks Drivas.

"Last night. There were four of us."

"And how many are there now?"

Liam pauses, hangs his head. "Three."

Drivas nods, an empathetic sadness to him. "You should leave now. You should go."

"Please." Liam takes another step, turns his focus to the

handgun, the throttle of the big man's hand around the grip. It shakes. The weapon ticks inside the motion.

"Stop," says Drivas. "No closer."

"You can shoot me. I don't care."

"Liam," springs Kate. "You don't mean that." She shifts to Drivas, shakes her head. "He doesn't mean that."

"I do," says Liam, speaking to her from his shoulder. "We're dead either way, right? We've both seen it."

"Don't say that," says Kate, the rising tears reflected in her voice. "That's not true."

"It is," affirms Drivas, drawing Kate's eyes from the ground. "I wish it weren't, but it is. If you've looked into the pool—"

"Did you?" interrupts Liam.

Drivas turns his face, refuses to meet their eyes.

"Answer me," urges Liam. "Please. Did you look?"

"Do not come to my home and push me—"

"Just answer the question," says Liam. "Please."

"I did," concedes Drivas, raising his chin. "So what? I looked. That doesn't change your fate."

"How does it not?" Liam's arms are out, incredulous. "If you beat it, so can we. It means we can undo this. We can fix it."

"You don't understand."

"Then explain it to us. We still have time, but our clocks are ticking just a little faster than average." Liam takes another step toward Drivas, pleading through his eyes. Drivas stares back down at Liam, this time relaxing on his weapon. He doesn't step away.

"Shit," says Drivas finally. "I don't want you on my land right now. I don't want you anywhere near me. But I'm also not a killer. I'm not going to shoot you. If it helps you leave faster, I'll tell you what I know. And then you leave. You go. You don't come back. That is my deal. You leave when we are done with our discussion."

Liam nods.

"We have a deal?"

"We have a deal," says Liam.

Drivas drops his head, swings around and walks inside. Behind him, Kate and Liam follow.

9

Detective Sideris perches on the sand, elbows cocked across her knees. A constant wind cuts down Kapari Beach, throwing grit against her neck and cheek, exposed beneath the upward sweep of hair, salt and pepper. The woman curses, covers up the chimney of her cup, shielding it from wayward grit.

She'd hardly touched her office when the call came in that morning, shortly after she'd released the young man and the woman from the precinct. The dispatcher had been strangely vague about the circumstances, or maybe they'd provided all the details that they could, but the pieces simply failed to fit together. Now that she'd arrived and saw things for herself, she understood completely, yet at the same time not at all.

The body of the man had been identified by his U.S. driver's license, found inside his wallet, inside the sling bag lying in the sand next to his chair.

Ethan Wallace

302 Mariners Arch, Chesapeake, Virginia

Inside the bag were two hundred euros, cell phone, passport, earbuds, towel, sunblock, two joints, a half-finished Coca-Cola, and a nearly finished bag of chips. Sideris moves as closely as she can without disruption of the scene, waiting out the photographer's final shots as he revolves around the subject, relying on the heavy telephoto lens to bring him close without encroachment. The sand has made this process touchy, not nearly as forgiving as more solid ground, perhaps a range of grass or patch of asphalt. Each step threatens to dislodge or bury evidence, be it prints or debris or whatever treasures lay within the sand, softly tufted everywhere except for where the body lay, packed hard where the blood has pooled and come together with the grains in red cohesion.

On the wind, the scent of copper finds her nose, the odor hard and spoiled. She turns to dodge it till it falls away again. She isn't typically affected by the scenes she visits. Twenty years in the profession's fortified her senses. Nasty shit often comes with the territory. Those who cannot hack it wash out early. She's lasted this long for a reason. But this one. . . she has no idea what this is.

Ethan Wallace, or what remains of him, is heaped up fetal on the sand, as if reverted to the womb, a last attempt to shield himself from whatever committed this. His abdomen is gone completely, spilling his remains across the sand, now coated in a mat of grit that turns them to a dull and shapeless wad. There are bites. Large chunks have been removed across most portions of the body: arms, legs, torso. Marks of teeth are well-defined, lines of their compression large and perforated, torn.

Six years back, she'd tended to the fallout of a shark attack. It hadn't been Kapari, but at another beach. Attacks aren't common in these parts, but happen on occasion. Memories of that scene have lingered with her. The brutality inflicted had made sure it stuck around inside her mind, likely wouldn't ever leave. The marks, the damage rendered to the victim, was near identical to what she sees today. Ethan Wallace has been torn to pieces, something that would, under proper circumstances, be chalked up to some few-and-far-between encounter here on the island. Some vicious rarity that's bound to happen at some point, to someone.

But circumstances weren't proper, as Ethan Wallace wasn't in the water. He had never been at any point, at least that anybody noticed. His body and his clothes are dry, further evidence that he'd not gone out, let alone the fact that if he had, and if even these wounds had been inflicted in the water, he'd not have made his way back to the shore. Not a chance in hell. It had all occurred right here, beside his chair, beside the woman lying next to him (now catatonic, with paramedics just beyond the dunes), who'd somehow maintained sleep until she'd come awake to catch the final act of what had happened, of what had still been taking place. She'd blacked out, remembering, reliably or not, that something utterly invisible had been taking him apart in front of her.

The photographer has finished up his shoot, is packing up his things, and Sideris takes the opportunity to move in closer, gain a better view of Ethan's body, the ground around him. The wind kicks up again, flinging sheets of sand across the body and its contents. White crystals lash their way across the crimson underlayment, and the action leads her eyes along the curvature of Ethan's back. White powder moves like clouds of smoke, catching on a scrawl of letters struck into the red, compacted sand. Sideris leans in close, reads the message.

Amor te ipsum.

She comes upright, whistles to the retreating backside of the cameraman. He turns, issues her a questioning nod. She reels him backward with her hand, points to the message in the sand.

"You get this?" She steps away, gives him visibility. "Right here. Make sure you get this."

"Don't see how I could've missed it."

"Please," says Sideris, pointing. "Let's be certain."

He frowns and pulls the camera from his bag.

Beyond the dunes, someone's crying, wailing now. An adult. There are children too. Tiny voices, stinging voices. She hates knowing what they've seen, hearing their reaction, hoping that they'd missed the premium view she had right now. This is nothing meant for children's eyes. Nothing meant for human eyes at all.

Overhead, seagulls scream. It's the only other sound.

Amor te ipsum.

Love thyself.

Sideris kneels again and wraps a palm across her mouth. This is no coincidence. She turns to a forensic tech that's stepping gingerly across the body.

"Make sure you get the phone, last contacts. Calls, texts.

Pull his passport, find out who he's here with, who he's been in contact with."

The technician nods acknowledgement and moves along. "Yes, ma'am."

Sideris lingers in her private thoughts.

Amor te ipsum. No coincidence.

She pulls her phone, pulls the contact, stares at the screen a moment. She rises to her feet, turns, and starts back toward the dunes.

10

Sebastian Drivas waves a hand across the center of the front room. "Sit."

Liam groups and clears a stack of newspapers from the only chair in the room, a thick recliner split by age in tiger stripes across its coffee-colored leather. He lays the papers on the hearth, looks up at Drivas in an effort to engage in small talk, ease the mood a little.

"Haven't seen one of these in years." Liam gestures toward the stack. "*TV Guide*, I mean. Not since I was a kid, I don't think."

Drivas takes his seat beside the papers on the bricks, sets the gun down next to him with an exasperated breath. "Seek and ye shall find. Internet is a glorious thing, isn't it?" He looks up at Liam, eyes cutting to the chase. "Ask your questions. I'll answer best I can, be helpful as I can. Unless you'd rather talk about this month's television schedule."

"No," says Liam. "No." He drops himself onto an

ottoman, offers Kate the recliner. For the first time, Liam notices the home is without windows. He moves his eyes around the space, realizing that it lacks all measure of reflective surface, be it glass, TV screens, doorknobs, picture frames, or so much as a dose of water left unsupervised inside a cup. Sebastian Drivas has clearly made a conscious effort to remove them from his home. What was once reflective at some point in time has since been muted, brushed or sanded, painted black or other finish, matte and unresponsive. He follows Liam's gaze and seems to read the thoughts that must've crossed his eyes as boldly telling as a teleprompter feed.

"Let's just say old habits die hard," says Drivas, now throwing glances of his own around the place, a look of rediscovery on his face. "Haven't thought about it in a while. Guess I kind of got used to it. All seems so normal now. Funny how that happens."

"What are we talking about right now?" asks Kate, confusedly observing now, herself.

"No reflective surfaces," says Liam. Drivas acknowledges this with a nod.

Kate seems to wither at the realization. "This is really real, isn't it? This is how we have to live our lives?" She looks like she could come apart. As if she could deconstruct in tears, in panic, on the verge of either, likely both.

"For you? No telling. I don't know you, anything about you."

"What does that mean?" she says. "You survived, but is this how? This is your life? How do you go through life like this? Without catching your reflection?"

"You'll do what you have to do, won't you?" says Drivas. "For me, I don't *have* to. For me, it's a choice. A safeguard."

"And for us?" says Liam.

"Like I said, I don't know you." Drivas moves a palm across his face, dumps a breath, and seeing their frustration, their confusion, continues. "Your friend, the one who died."

"Gemma," says Kate. "She was my best friend."

"Gemma. Okay. Where this Gemma was found, what were the circumstances?"

"Strangulation." Kate shakes her head defeatedly. "None of it makes any sense."

"The environment around her," says Drivas. "It was unchanged, yes? Unremarkable."

"Yes," frowns Kate. "The water line. The one that choked her, it was untouched. Everything was." She pauses, considers this, makes the correction. "Almost everything."

"There was a message, yes?"

"*Amor te ipsum*," whispers Kate.

Drivas nods. "Love thyself. You understand Narcissus, yes? Who he was?"

"Yeah," says Kate. "But there are many stories."

"Narcissus governs the reflective world. It is where he lives. He cannot cross to ours, but he can manipulate the world inside the reflection." He drags a set of nails across the range of stubble on his cheek. "The laws of our world don't apply in his. They're warped, only partly functional."

"I'm not following," says Liam.

"Your friend was strangled with the water line, but the water line remained untouched."

"That's right."

"In *our* world."

He sees realization dawn across their faces.

"But Gemma, her death," says Kate. "Gemma *wasn't* untouched. She's gone now. He killed her. That's here, on our side, in our world."

"He was bound to her, a part of her," says Drivas. "Tethered to her very soul through her reflection."

"This shit is making my damn head hurt," says Liam. "I'm just having a bit of a hard time here, sorry."

"To put it simply, you are infected," says Drivas.

"What?"

"When you looked into the pool, your reflection was infected. He attached himself to it, to you. He embedded himself, became one with you. You are carriers, and he is a malignance."

"So, it's all true," says Liam. "All of it. The legends. The stuff about Narcissus trading off his soul for immortality, winding up confined to the pool, trapped there forever."

"Unless someone comes along, offers him a means to escape," says Kate, a troubling numbness playing on the surface of her eyes.

Drivas nods.

"But why?" asks Liam. "It doesn't make any sense. If he's escaped, why kill off the host that liberates him?"

"It is his intolerance of insecurity that drives his wrath," says Drivas. "His lust for perfection. Those who harbor some degree of insecurity, who are by any measure dissatisfied with themselves, flawed by self-perception, are at risk. The carrier will be judged."

Kate spits against the backside of her teeth. "That's ridiculous."

"How so?"

"It's an impossible standard," says Kate. "It makes no sense."

Drivas holds on that consideration, then lifts a hand as if to pause the moment, continues. "You might compare it to Christian teachings. Jesus was man and God in one, but he was required to be spotless as a man, as God could not possibly dwell in the presence of sin. Does that make sense to you?" Drivas studies their expressions. "Narcissus equally cannot dwell in the presence of insecurity. It runs counter to his very nature. It is not possible, and so he destroys his unclean host as a result. Such a host is useless to him."

"How do you even know this stuff?" asks Liam through an unintentional glare. He's somehow struck by memories of his brother, long forgotten until now, pinning him against the dirt with one knee in his back, a quarter in his hand, ready for the flip.

Watch it spin, lose or win!

He feels the knee against his spine, hot tears against his cheeks.

Quarter's king! Heads or tails? What's it gonna be? Take your licks or hit the bricks!

"I've had a lot of time to read, son," says Drivas, frowning to himself. "More time than you can comprehend."

The memory falls away. Liam hardly registers what Drivas says. His brother's knee still jams itself against his spine.

"But when you say anyone that might bear some insecurity," chuffs Kate, almost shouting now in her bewilderment, "that's *everyone*, right? Someone. . . someone would almost have to. . . to be *inhuman* to not feel insecurity in one way or another."

"Not everyone," says Drivas. His head is down, and he brings a thumb and index finger to his brow, twists the flesh with punishing deliberation.

"You're saying *that's* how you survived? That's why everyone in your group died except for you?" Kate releases an incredulous huff of air. "Or did you even look into the pool?" Her tone is frantic in her disbelief, her unwillingness to accept what he is telling her, the seeming impossibility of their survival. "Were you even there? Did you even—"

"I was there. I tell you, I looked," growls Drivas. The muscles squirm along his jaw, and his eyes appear to lose their color, overcast and darker in the face of Kate's haphazard accusations. "Don't you come into my home and question my integrity."

"Hey, whoa," says Liam, not entirely sure if he is calming Kate, or Drivas, maybe both. He looks to Kate and lays his hand on hers. "Okay, nobody's questioning your integrity. She's just scared. We both are. We need help; however you can give it."

"I already told you it's out of my hands. It's out of your hands, too. It's a matter of character, of self-fulfillment. If you're not happy, *truly* happy with yourself, then he will know. He will sniff it out like a cadaver dog and tear your soul to pieces for it."

Kate is having trouble sitting still, and her restlessness is making Liam nervous. Drivas already doesn't want them there, and Kate is well en route to making sure they aren't. He tries not to lock eyes with the man, but in his peripheral, he can see the large man watching Kate, mindfully waiting for some reason to eject them both.

"Your place," agrees Liam, wanting nothing greater than

to navigate their talk to calmer seas. "But if you're fully cured, no longer possessed, why still live like this?"

Drivas frowns, and Liam is afraid the words have come out wrong, not as intended.

"No," starts Liam, "what I mean is—"

"I know what you mean," severs Drivas, rising to his feet. He crosses the room, and Liam watches as he does, half expecting him to open up the door, ask for them to leave. Instead, he hooks a right into the kitchen. They hear the seal release on the refrigerator door, then suck closed again. They hear the carbonated sniff as he uncaps a beer and flicks the cap onto the counter. It clatters to a stop, and they wait in silence as he drinks, listening to the long and squelching movements of his throat before they stop and Drivas reappears inside the kitchen entry. He seems buried in his thoughts, and Liam wonders if the intention of his question really hadn't quite been understood when Drivas gets to speaking once again.

"You remember what I said about old habits dying hard?"

Liam nods, "Yeah." He catches Kate in his peripheral. She isn't squirming anymore, a good thing. But she's also seemed to take another route, having fallen into catatonic silence. Her eyes are on her hands again, rolling over in her lap. It unsettles him.

"I've seen no signs of it in thirty years." Sebastian Drivas hauls his shoulder from the jamb and leaves the entry, settling on a table's edge beside the chair instead. "But I fear it will return. I fear it waits for me, and so I take precautions."

"But you survived before. It didn't bother you then. You passed the test, right?"

"Back then, I was, eh. . ." Drivas hesitates, makes movements with his hand, spinning through the air in a vocabularic hunt.

"Arrogant?"

Liam turns to Kate, face twisted in spasmodic disbelief. She doesn't notice, having not removed her eyes from where they rest.

Drivas shakes his head, lets his hand fall from the air, abandoning its attempt at flight. "That is it," he concedes. "That would be the word."

"A narcissist, maybe?"

"Kate," warns Liam. She is staring back at Drivas now, unsatisfied with where he's left them, without any measure of support or usable advice for someone who's already been where they are, fought a fight in which nobody else could stand a chance of helping, let alone believing in the first place.

"Maybe." Drivas seems to measure the suggestion as he lets his head fall both ways on his neck. "Very possible. But to the point you try to make, I beat it then. I escaped, yes. Satisfied it, whatever. But now I am much older. And with time, with that age comes certain insecurities. Insecurities I did not have back then. The ego, it decomposes with the years. It ages like the rest of us, breaks down." He draws a breath and lays his head back on his neck, stares into the ceiling. "You understand? I do not believe I'd fare so well these days. And so, I take precautions."

Drivas gives himself a moment, tries to swallow down the tide of grief that has begun to rise.

"I lost my friends," he continues. "I lost my life to that. . . that *thing*." His voice is shaking now. "Tragedy, loss, guilt;

these things will break a human being, change them, make them pray for death. You say that I survived. Did I?"

"You did, though," says Liam quietly. "You don't have to live this way. It wasn't your fault."

"Fault. A very human word. But it does not care. It is not concerned with fault, with blame. It is a judge, and my friends were punished for their humanity, their vulnerabilities, while I... I was *rewarded* for my," Drivas laughs, swings his head disgustedly, gestures toward Kate, "my *narcissism,* as you say."

"I didn't mean," starts Kate, wishing she could roll the moments back, surgically extract the words she'd spoken out of anger, frustration.

"You did. You meant it. And that is okay, because it's the truth." He lets out a breath and slumps against his arms, tent poles rooted to his knees. "What can I say, hm? It is the truth, and you speak it plainly." Drivas aims a hefty pointer at her. "I admire that, young lady."

Kate works her mouth into a slant as she begins to gnaw the inside of her cheek. The three of them have fallen into silence, each one waiting out the next, unsure of where to go from here. Liam moves to speak, to cut the silence when his phone begins to vibrate in his pocket. He slips it free, finds the screen illuminated by a local number. He recognizes it as the one Detective Sideris used to call him to the station earlier that morning. Liam excuses himself and steps out front.

"Who is it?" follows Kate. Liam shakes the question off and gestures her back to her seat.

"Not sure," he lies. "Give me a sec."

Kate lingers at the center of the living room with both

arms tied across her chest as Liam leaves her for the front porch, pulling shut the door behind him.

Place two strangers in a room together in a time of stress and observe what happens to the focus of attention. A protective bubble starts to form, salvaged from the fragments of their small talk, topics of discussion that are safe and friendly. It rises like a shield between them and the present threat, as if to pass through what they'd built would strip the menace of its bite. It's an innate habit of adaptation, technique of survival, the reason why Kate finally had begun to speak to Drivas, facing down her fear through redirection versus suffocating underneath its weight in silence. The reason, at the time Liam had returned from the front porch, Drivas had been in the middle of a story having something to do with fishing from the rocky coast and how the crabs that stripped his hooks of bait were found to be more tasty than the fish he'd originally set out to catch, prompted by another line of discussion centered around Kate's planned thesis on the relative contribution of the blue crab. The shield collapsed when they looked up at Liam's entry, saw the blood had fled his face. His eyes possessed a doll-like vacancy that thwarted movement toward the others. Instead, they focused on a table lamp that ticked against the body of a fly that sought escape, pinned beneath the shade as if some kind of cruel and blinding habitat.

Seeing Liam, Kate feels her hands and feet go cold, and nearly doesn't want to breathe for fear of destabilizing what might bind his silence. She doesn't want to know what he knows, what makes him look that way. She doesn't want to join him in that place, and if she could put him on a raft and shove him out to sea to be sure she never would, she feels in that moment that she'd do it without hesitation.

"You have lost another," says Drivas. He's looking at his hands, a cluster in his lap. It's a statement of fact, not a question.

Liam finally lifts his eyes up to the room, stains of lamplight pulsing at the darkest regions of his vision.

His silence presses Kate as if a needle that resists the flesh. "Liam?" Kate turns to Drivas. "Why would you say that? What the actual fuck is wrong with you?"

Drivas hangs his head, refuses to look at either of them.

"Liam, why aren't you saying anything?" Kate's voice is surging now, louder by the syllable. "Why would you let him say something like that? Tell him Ethan's fine. Tell him it's not Ethan." Kate is almost choking on her words. They begin to crumble at the last, slowing down, escaping loud and soft at once beneath the rising tide that throttles portions of their structure. She sounds like a talking doll with fading batteries.

Liam's head begins to wag. "They found him on the beach."

"Liam, no," hisses Kate. Her voice has left her. She shakes her head, a motion with no sign of stopping. "No, that's not true."

"They traced him to us through his passport."

Kate is losing it. Her mouth hangs wide and silent. The loss of Gemma, now Ethan, together finally splits the gates, enters her, and begins to rut the grief from deep inside and haul it to the surface. It comes too fast, a giant hand that grips the room and throws it spinning. Kate's body loses its integrity, keeling to the side against the leather armrest of the chair.

Slowly, Liam turns, a blunted movement, still parsing out what he's been told, the present moment in the room, what to feel, what to say, at a loss for either as his senses numb and leave him idling neutral.

Drivas turns and lifts Kate gently, slips a pillow underneath her shoulder, her head. "Rest. It's going to be okay. Just rest." The words are empty, meaningless, crafted from the same thing as the hasty shield of small talk they'd erected only moments prior. He turns to Liam.

"It is so, then. Another has been taken."

Liam nods.

"And the words," says Drivas. "They were there, as well."

"Written in the sand," whispers Liam. "In the blood, in the sand." His voice has found its way back to the dreamlike state he'd held the first time that he'd looked into the pool, the cobalt shimmer of the limestone constellations, the darkened sockets of himself.

"I am sorry for your loss, young man."

"They want to speak to us," says Liam. His eyes are hollow, helpless. They beg the man for guidance, for answers, for anything that he can offer. "The police. They want us to come and talk to them."

Drivas nods. "As they did with me."

"But we can't tell them. They would never believe us."

"No, they won't," says the man. He works his hands against each other, watches his fingers turn across his palms, over, under, over. "Especially knowing you have spoken with me. They will suspect we have conspired."

"But they don't know that. They won't even know we came to see you."

"They will," says Drivas. "I assure you they are triangulating your location as we speak. You need to go to them before things get worse for you. Tell them your truth. *Our* truth."

"You said it yourself," pleads Liam. "They won't believe us. They'll lock us up on insanity alone!"

"You don't have a choice. The truth is all you have at this point, just as it was all *I* had."

"We'll be completely exposed." Liam's hands are in his hair, and he holds onto his head as if it's on the verge of falling from his body. "They won't be able to protect us. We won't even be able to protect ourselves."

Drivas speaks to Liam with the calm and even-keeled demeanor of a father to his frightened son. "Listen to me. Do you plan on dodging your reflections for the rest of your lives? Is that your plan?"

Liam runs his hands across his head. He looks around the home, considers its nonreflective sterility.

He follows Liam's gaze. "Is this life?" Drivas throws his palms into the air. "For me, this is a choice, not a necessity. I survived because he found me worthy of existence, not because I was able to avoid my reflection for the rest of my life. If that is your plan, you are a fool. You might as well be dead."

Behind them, Kate lets out a sound. She leans forward on her hands, elbows pitched into her quads. She mumbles something, muffled, too low for them to hear.

"You have no choice," reinforces Drivas. "None. You need to go now. Both of you."

"Go where," asks Kate. She pulls her face up from the cradle of her palms, lets it hover there. "Where are we supposed to go?"

"He's right, Kate." Liam swipes a hand across his mouth and nose, shakes his head. "We're going to Sideris."

His words are resurrective as a pack of smelling salts. Kate comes to her feet at once and joins the two men in one long, impatient stride. She throws her eyes from one man to the other, wondering if they've lost their minds completely. "What the hell did I miss?"

"That was Sideris on the line, Kate. She wants to see us. If we don't go, if we run, they're going to find us, bring us in. They'll think we had something to do with this."

Kate rocks on her legs, wraps her torso tight beneath her arms, finally asks the question as her face begins to deconstruct again. "What happened to Ethan?"

Liam falters, unsure how to answer, if he even should. He feels something sting the backside of his throat, a blade held like a threat against his voice. He swallows, washes back the rising grief. "We'll talk about it later. With Sideris. Might be best to wait till then anyway."

She doesn't argue with him, comfortable in her ignorance. "But, he's gone," says Kate. "He's actually gone. She told you that."

Liam nods. "Yeah," he whispers. "He is."

And then Kate begins to cry again, but this time they leave the house, walk out to the waiting car, Drivas guiding with his hand, large and heavy, empathetically positioned at the center of her back.

11

Everything had seemed to dim the slightest bit, first with Gemma, then with Ethan. It seemed as if the world around them had been filtered somehow, a bit like looking through a dirty drinking glass, what lay beyond the glass made unclean just the same. Liam feels this strongly, though he keeps it to himself. He knows it all is in his head, some psychological distortion triggered by their loss. It's as though a clock has been kicked into motion, initiation of their own demise, counting down in heightened shades of gray until the image would eventually die completely, fully dark. Liam shakes the notion from his mind and brings himself around again, focused on the real, the now, the necessary.

"What exactly are we going to tell them, Liam?" Kate has calmed along the way. She'd reserve her grief until a later time when she could grieve alone, or maybe they could grieve together. For now, they'll have to reign it in, get their minds in order. They're already going to have a hell of a time relaying what they know, no doubt labeled crazy before half the story had been told. Then there is the federal trespassing charge that may or may not come, but that worry also would be stashed away for later. For now, they'll only move to bring an end to what is happening, even if that meant they'd die trying. They're likely going to die regardless. This thing is carried on them like a sickness. It is part of them at this point, for better or for worse.

"We tell them the truth. We tell them everything," says Liam. "We do that, and we know we've done the best we can. We've kept nothing to ourselves, you know?"

Kate doesn't answer, still walking next to him, still unsure, just wanting this whole thing to end, to be done. She wants to go back home. To go back to her life, pretend she'd never come here, had never even met Gemma, met Ethan, met Liam. To erase it all and start again. It's a selfish, shitty wish, but it is hers, and it is honest. She'd give anything to make it so.

"I think we're going to be okay, and this is the first step," says Liam as they climb the marble steps toward the glass doors of the Mykonos Police Department. "Coming clean with what we know."

Kate looks at Liam, smooths her lips into a subtle line. Something to appease him. Something to make him stop the pep talk. She's not stupid. And for all she knows, maybe Liam actually *has* been duped by his own lie. And if that's the case, then good for him. If he takes some pathetic comfort in that, then who is she to shit all over it? In all sincerity, good for him. Next to her first wish, she could wish for such naivety as well. That would be a good wish, more realistic, less shitty. Yes, a good wish.

Her trance is severed by a wall of icy air that hits her as they cross the threshold to the precinct lobby. Sideris is already waiting for them, seated in a plastic wall-mount bucket seat, legs toppled over one another. She unwinds her legs and rises slowly, wasting no more breath than what it takes to speak their names, and leads them through another door that opens with a stroke across the air with her proximity badge.

"We will, of course, be separating you," says Sideris, slowing as two officers emerge behind her.

Like some chemical reaction, what temporary calmness Kate has managed falls apart on contact with the woman's words, and her eyes go wide and frantic. "No, wait. You just wanted to talk to us. You said. . . you said you just wanted to talk."

"And I do, but we interrogate you independently of each other, let you tell your stories separately, see what doesn't quite add up, see what does. You know. It is protocol."

"Fuck your protocol!" Kate blurts. She turns to Liam, eyes wild and aching for support.

"Kate, it's fine," says Liam, visibly disquieted. "Just talk to them. Tell them what you know. I'll do the same. We have nothing to hide. You know this."

"No, Liam. Fuck that. Don't you see what they're doing?" Kate begins to back away, butting up against an officer behind her. He places one hand on her arm, shaken off as if a roach has crawled into her sleeve. "Don't fucking touch me. I want a lawyer. I have the right to an attorney."

Sideris dumps a breath. "You are not on U.S. soil. Your rights do not apply here."

"Kate, just get this over with. You're acting like a guilty person."

Kate's face has melted into an incredulous expression. She looks from Liam to Sideris, back again, swings her head in disbelief.

"We are not arresting you, Ms. Porter." Sideris motions toward her. "Please. We only wish to speak, to find out what you know. Find out what happened to your friend. Surely you don't think that we believe you tore his body up yourself. That you disemboweled him on a public beach, in plain sight."

Liam shuts his eyes, curses underneath his breath.

"Tore him up?" blinks Kate, completely at a loss for comprehension of the woman's words. "Disemboweled?!" Her breaths began to hitch inside her throat, and she stumbles back against the wall.

"You did not know," says Sideris. She turns to Liam with accusatory flair. "You did not tell her?"

"No. I didn't."

"I might have handled this more carefully, had I known." The detective puts a hand up to her mouth, pulls her lips together in an exercise of thought, then sets them free. "Okay, come along. We talk now."

Kate doesn't resist, lifted from the wall as no more a human than a doll collected from a daycare floor.

"We will speak with Ms. Porter first, then you," says Sideris as they walk the hall. "We have a room for you to wait."

Liam offers her a half-nod, then calls out to Kate before

Sideris walks her through the far door at hall's end.

"Kate."

Kate turns, but not completely, the way the blind might angle one ear toward a sound.

"The truth. And be aware of your reflection."

Sideris frowns, puzzled by the comment, then turns and leads the young woman into the interrogation room.

Relief hits Liam as he walks into his waiting quarters. The chairs are polymer, bolted to the floor with matte steel feet. The table is of laminate construction, matte as well with seashell designs across its surface. There is no television, no mirror, no glass or other surface through which his reflection might derive its access. Kate is out of his control, on her own. She'll have to look out for herself. But for now, he is safe, and all he has to do is wait.

Detective Sideris leans back in her chair. The room is quiet, save the subtle exchange of whistling breaths between them both. She pulls a brushed steel Zippo from her pocket, strikes the flint, holds it to the cigarette that dangles from her wind-chapped lips. She sucks the flame, forming cirrus clouds between herself and Kate.

Sideris notices Kate's attention on the lighter. She turns it over in her hand. "Ten-year anniversary with the department. A gift. Has our logo on the front. See?" She smooths her thumb across the image, leaves it on the table.

"Mhm," Kate nods.

"I'm sorry. It's the cigarette, isn't it? I don't mean to be inconsiderate," says Sideris, lowering the cigarette onto a plastic ashtray in the center of the table. "I forgot your U.S. laws forbid public smoking."

"But we're not on U.S. soil, are we?"

"Touché," says Sideris. She cocks her head, bumps a lump of ash into the dish. "I deserve that."

Kate clears her throat, binds her arms. "Only inside."

Sideris lifts her brow. "Pardon?"

"U.S. law."

"Ah," the woman nods. "I see. Technically, laws are same in Greece. But, you know. . ." She twitches the cigarette between her fingers, gestures toward it with her other hand. "And you? Does it bother?"

"It's fine," mumbles Kate, squeezing both words through her near-clenched teeth. She just wants out, to go home, forget this place all together.

"Good. Okay."

Sideris breathes, long and heavy, holds on Kate a moment, connecting with her eyes. "I apologize for catching you off-guard with what I said out there. About your friend, how he passed. That was wrong of me. I didn't know that you were unaware. I only assumed—"

Kate shakes it off, breaks the explanation short. "That's on Liam. He should have told me." The words come quicker, sharper than intended, emergence of resentment that had taken shape without her knowledge. But she is angry. He had no right to keep that to himself. She feels the stone rise in her throat, lodge itself in place, an ugly mass designed to break her. She would not let it, especially in the presence of this woman. "I'm fine. It's fine. Let's talk. And I want to know what happened. I want to know everything."

"Okay, well then," says Sideris. She pulls a sleeve of paperwork against the table's edge, flips it open. "That makes two of us, Ms. Porter. I want to believe your hands are clean, that you had nothing to do with any of this, but I cannot help but wonder what you're keeping from me." The woman's eyes reduce themselves, and she leans onto the table. "And I know you're holding something back."

"That's why we're here, Detective," says Kate. "For you to know what we know, as incredibly insane as it might sound."

Sideris slowly falls back in her chair, ties her arms across her chest. "Okay?" The cigarette juts from her fingers like a smoldering thorn. "Would this insanity somehow be related to Sebastian Drivas?" Her brow goes up on one side, as if the statement is a certain *gotcha* that would bind Kate's tongue, draw the perspiration to her flesh.

"You might say that."

Kate's readiness disarms Sideris of her bite. The admission is an unexpected twist of reckoning. "Go on," says Sideris. She jams the cigarette against her teeth and pulls a long and patient drag.

"We tracked him down because he's the only one who knows what we're dealing with. The only one who might be able to help somehow."

"Helping is *our* job, Ms. Porter. You need help, you come to us."

"This one's outside your jurisdiction," says Kate.

"It would work in your favor to comply, to not insult me, Ms. Porter." Sideris turns the cigarette inside her palm and breaks its back against the bottom of the tray. The orange ember lets out one last breath before it dies completely, unfurling toward the ceiling like a ribbon in reverse.

In the corner of the room, a security camera watches both in silence. Shielded by an onyx dome, something stirs against the high-gloss surface.

"I don't say that as an insult, Detective. I promise," says Kate. "When I tell you what we know, you're going to think we're crazy, question our sanity, just like what happened to Sebastian Drivas when he came clean with what he knew thirty-two years ago. He tried to tell them, but nobody believed him. But it's real. All of it. I promise you."

Sideris stares at Kate, stone-faced. "This is. . . some kind of copycat thing? A recreation of what happened to those people. To Drivas's friends? Does he have something to do with this?"

Kate snuffs. "Of course not."

In the fish-eyed universe sprawled out across the dome, standing opposite reality but tethered to it nonetheless, Kate's reflection leans across the table, takes the lighter in its hand.

Response had been delayed. The sprinklers in the room had failed. Investigators later would discover that the head had been irreparably corroded, sabotaging function. They would also find a message etched in soot and ash across the wall. How it got there would remain a mystery, taken as confession of a dying woman, spontaneously and inexplicably combusted. Surveillance ultimately would fail to capture those last moments, blinded by the smoke.

When Liam hears commotion in the halls, the shouting, the beat of rubber soles, wet and squalling on the tile; when the burning smell, the screams begin to reach him where he sits, he doesn't bother moving. When the sprinkler ruptures overhead, forms a mushroom cap of water that descends upon the room, he doesn't budge.

Kate is gone. Judgement has been rendered.

He knows it. He feels it.

The water falls on him in torrents. Still, he waits. It is all that he can do. Somewhere, a coin has flipped. Heads and tails, turning over, spinning toward impending judgement. Liam sits there at the table, his deadpan gaze set on its surface. The water gathers underneath his face, many parts connecting as a whole. And as it does, he begins to see himself.

A coin is spinning, spinning, falling toward his judgement.

Take your licks or hit the bricks!

He watches his reflection, floating on the sheet of water. His reflection watches him in turn. There is something in the eyes, the sockets, bruised and sleepless, selfish and entitled, qualities that Liam questions, true reflection of himself or something else.

All else falls away, his own survival standing paramount to everything they have endured. It is the prize awaiting on the far side of the coming moment. Hope blooms inside the darkness.

He stares into the soiled eyes of his reflection, and his reflection weighs him in return.

Together, they wait.

ACKNOWLEDGMENTS

Writing is an inherently solitary, lengthy, and frequently discouraging pursuit, and I'm eternally thankful for the time and support my wonderful wife and children have given me throughout the countless hours of imagination-chasing across the keyboard. Without that enduring patience, understanding, and encouragement day and night, you wouldn't be holding this book in your hands right now. A tremendous thank you to my mom and dad for always encouraging me to chase my writerly ambitions from a very early age, and continuing to do so today.

Thank you to Alan Lastufka and Shortwave Publishing for your unparalleled professionalism, courtesy, and outstanding ease of collaboration throughout the entire publishing process. You've made this experience a dream, and for that I'm so grateful. Thank you to Nancy LaFever and Erin Foster for your editorial and proofreading expertise, through which this book was honed to its finest possible edge.

I'd like to thank Clay McLeod Chapman and everyone else who read and reviewed Narcissus. It is truly appreciated, and I feel so fortunate to have received your support.

Lastly, I'd like to pay special thanks to Brendan Deneen

for being such a tireless, supportive, and knowledgeable advocate in the world of film and television. I consider myself exceedingly fortunate to have your representation and look forward to what opportunities lay ahead.

ABOUT THE AUTHOR

Adam Godfrey is a novelist and author of short stories. His genre-crossing work ranges from speculative to horrific, frequently drawing upon historical, technological, and scientific elements to create content which effectively blurs the lines between the plausible and implausible.

Adam holds over twenty years of experience working for the United States Department of Defense in information technology and cybersecurity risk management. He holds a master's degree in cybersecurity, and his professional contributions to the field have been internationally featured across a variety of media platforms.

Having Attention Deficit Disorder (ADD), Adam is a passionate advocate for encouraging others living with neurodiversity to leverage strengths of their conditions toward personal and professional success.

He currently lives with his family in Chesapeake, Virginia.

A NOTE FROM
SHORTWAVE PUBLISHING

Thank you for reading *Narcissus*!

If you enjoyed it, please consider writing a review or telling a friend! Word-of-mouth helps readers find more titles they may enjoy and that, in turn, helps us continue to publish more titles like this.

∽

OUR WEBSITE
shortwavepublishing.com

SOCIAL MEDIA
@ShortwaveBooks

EMAIL US
contact@shortwavepublishing.com